Immortal Remains

ROOK HASTINGS

W0006720

CW00868098

HarperCollins *Children's Books*

First published in Great Britain by
HarperCollins *Children's Books* in 2010

HarperCollins *Children's Books* is a division of
HarperCollins*Publishers* Ltd,
77-85 Fulham Palace Road, Hammersmith, London, W6 8JB.

1

ISBN 978-0-00-725811-6

Typeset by Palimpsest Book Production Limited, Falkirk, Stirlingshire

For Lily, Harry and Fred

PROLOGUE

*H*ashim's eyes snapped open. He'd heard something, he was sure he had heard something. All the tiny hairs on his arms and the back of his neck stood up on end, his heart shuddering as if something he couldn't quite remember had frightened him awake.

He stared into the impenetrable darkness while he waited for his eyes to adjust to the dense black. Under his bedroom door was a thin sliver of light from the bulb on the landing. Hashim stared hard at it, remembering when he was little and afraid of things that go bump in the night how he'd clutch on to his teddy and bury his head under the covers. That was when he believed his mum and dad when they told him ghosts weren't real. Now he knew the truth, and almost everywhere he looked he saw a dead person staring back at him.

But not here, not in his bedroom. They'd never come in here yet; here he was safe, he was normal. As Hashim took long deep breaths, the darkness around him eased and he could make out some familiar shapes in his room.

The chair in the corner covered in clothes, his wardrobe door left open, stuff spilling out on to the cluttered carpet. He pushed himself up on his elbows and waited for his heart to slow down. He was being silly. Whatever it was that had terrified him must be in his head. The frenzied thumping in his chest must mean he'd been dreaming again; of cold dead hands grasping for him, and screams he couldn't hear but that threatened to boil his brain. And although he couldn't remember the nightmare that had startled him awake, Hashim thought it was a pretty safe bet that he'd been dreaming of Emily again. Emily had been the class victim; dowdy, boring, pale – open season when it came to bullying, and by the time he'd finally got to know her, she'd been dead for several weeks. Hashim had been hanging around with a ghost. But he'd only discovered this when he found Emily's blackened corpse, twisted in permanent anguish, in a burnt-out Mini Metro under the overpass.

It wasn't Emily's ghost that had frightened him. It was the image of how he had found her that kept haunting his dreams. Her face... no eyes... just empty hollows, her expression contorted in a scream... Hashim's stomach lurched and he pressed the back of his hand to his mouth as he tasted last night's tea, bitter on the back of his tongue. He'd seen the reality of death with his own eyes; he'd smelt it, tasted it even. And for the first time he'd realised what it meant, what all of the hundreds of ghosts around him meant. That for each and every one of them, somewhere there was a grave containing a body that used to have a heartbeat; that used to breathe and run and laugh just like him.

But that corpse wasn't Emily, Hashim told himself, squeezing his eyes tightly shut as if he could block out the image he knew was locked inside his head forever. Emily made it to the other side to be with her mother, thanks to him and the others too. The army of ghosts had tried to trap them all that night, but they hadn't got to her, so she wasn't caught forever in constant fear and pain, forced to march with a legion of hate-filled ghosts while her body rotted under six feet of damp worm-infested earth.

Emily's spirit was free. For a fleeting moment, Hashim envied his dead friend. He couldn't remember the last time he'd felt safe, the last time he hadn't looked up to see someone dead looking back at him, or the last time he'd woken up without that nagging feeling that very soon something terrible was going to happen – and that when it did, there would be nothing he could do to stop it.

Hashim concentrated on the slice of yellow light under his bedroom door. He could hear his mum's snores, gently rumbling from up the hallway, and the telly still on downstairs, which his dad would have fallen asleep in front of hours ago. Somewhere his brother, Farid, would be on the phone to his girlfriend, talking into the early hours even though they'd seen each other all day at work.

"My life is ordinary," Hashim said out loud as he focused on the light coming under his door. "I'm just an ordinary, normal, nobody kid."

A shadow briefly cut across the light; Farid probably, or Dad dragging himself up to bed at last. But instead of feeling comforted, Hashim was suddenly on edge again. Something wasn't right. The boards on the stairs were deathly quiet. No creaks, no footsteps. No sound at all.

Hashim drew his bed covers up against his chest. One, two, then maybe twenty or more shadows flitted rapidly by, each one obliterating the light for a second. Slowly Hashim reached out to switch the lamp on by his bed, but his hand froze in mid-air. There was a pair of feet stood on the other side of the door, two columns of shadow cutting into that reassuring band of light. Someone was waiting on the other side.

Then the handle on the bedroom door rattled.

"No," Hashim whispered.

The handle rattled again, vigorously, violently. Hashim pushed himself back into his pillow. His bedroom wasn't locked, there was no bolt. A human, an *alive* human would have just walked in.

"You can't come in." Hashim tried to speak, but his voice was hoarse, broken, imprisoned in his throat.

The door handle rattled once more, but this time it seemed as if the whole room was shaking. The glass of water on the chest of drawers next to his bed vibrated so hard it slid across the surface, and the remote for his PlayStation toppled to the floor. Books juddered off their shelves, crashing down one by one.

Someone should've woken up, but no one did. Then just as suddenly, an all-encompassing silence blanketed everything, filling Hashim's ears with thick quiet, and slowly, very slowly, Hashim's bedroom door swung open.

"P...p... please," he stuttered.

For a second the hallway was empty, the solitary bulb burning brightly in the night.

And then they were there. The army of the dead.

Silently they walked forwards, their empty eyes fixed on him, anger and unheard screams filling every ounce of

11

silence with menace. An old woman first, just like any old lady you'd see at the bus stop, with her handbag over her arm. But her face was grey, the spark of who she might once have been gone forever. A little boy next, his football printed with the Arsenal emblem still tucked under one arm. Then a man in a suit and tie, still clutching a briefcase in his bony hand. They kept coming in, gathering around the bed.

"Go away," Hashim pleaded. "Leave me alone!"

The little boy reached out and tugged at the duvet with tiny, icy fingers.

"*No!*" Hand after hand started reaching for him, their freezing cold touch sending icy shivers searing through his veins. It was death; death was touching him, death had sent all these souls to find him, to catch him and drag him back with them.

"No! No, no, no, no, no..." Hashim fought, his arms flailing wildly as the hands plucked at his clothes, his skin, his hair. "Please... *leave me alone!*"

"Hashim! Wake up, you nutter!" Farid's voice transformed the room. One second it was pitch-black and full of murderous ghosts, the next filled with watery sunlight streaming in through drawn curtains. "Man, what were you dreaming about? You were screaming like a girl, bruv, seriously."

Hashim looked around, blinking in the bright light,

uncertain which was real: the dark, frightening night he had just been dragged out of, or this bright, untidy room soaked in daylight.

"I don't know, bad dream, I guess," Hashim said.

"Yeah, well. Get your sorry backside out of bed, yeah? Otherwise it'll be Mum who'll be making you scream for mercy." Shaking his head, Farid turned to leave then stumbled over something, swearing loudly.

"And another thing, don't leave your footballs lying around where anyone can fall over them." Farid picked up the ball and chucked it hard at Hashim's head. "And since when have you supported Arsenal?"

Hashim stared at the ball in his lap, horror welling up inside his chest. He wouldn't be seen dead supporting Arsenal.

It belonged to the little ghost boy; a soldier in the army of the dead.

CHAPTER ONE

"*T*his is about everything that we know is going on in Woodsville but that everyone pretends we don't see. Got a story no one else believes? Seen something you can't explain? Message me at shadowgirl@ woodsvillehigh.com to share. Send me photos, footage and evidence and I'll post it here. Something's going on and I'm going to find out what. How do I know? Because a few weeks ago, I found that one of my best friends was dead. Her name was Emily Night..."

Kelly shook her head as she read the print-out of Bethan's blog.

"Bethan, are you mad? Why don't you just write 'please kick me, I'm a moron' on your forehead if you want to commit school suicide? At least it'd be quicker and less painful. And as for Shadowgirl? Bloody hell, Beth."

"I'm not mad," Bethan scowled. "That's the whole point." She glanced at Jay who was sitting across the café table from them, looking out of the window at the dull, spring afternoon. The bright pink blossom-laden trees outside were stark against the grey of everything else in Woodsville, including the people. He looked like he was waiting for someone he didn't especially want to see.

When Jay had sent her a text to meet him in the café, Bethan had half hoped it would be just the two of them, so she could talk about her blog and the research she'd done without Kelly weighing in. Even so, becoming friends with Kelly was one of the best things that had ever happened to Bethan. After years of mooching down the school corridors alone, looking like she didn't give a rat's arse about anyone else, Bethan finally had a friend. A cool friend, who'd sit next to her at lunch or be her partner in Chemistry – if she ever showed up to class. The downside to being Kelly's friend was that other people, not especially nice people, had started noticing her. Bethan knew that Kelly was just trying to make sure she survived the scrutiny by pointing out her flaws, but that meant becoming a different person; more like Kelly and her old crew. Bethan wasn't sure she could do that.

"Look," she told Kelly. "Everyone knows what happened with Emily. But no one else will admit it. Look at them!"

Kelly followed Bethan's nod to some other Woodsville High girls in the café. It was a popular haunt; one of the few places that didn't insist on only two teenagers in at a time, or that drinks had to be paid for up-front. The girls were laughing, chatting, messing around like normal. But Bethan couldn't shake the feeling that they were circling like wild animals sizing up their prey, preparing for a kill. And she had a horrible feeling that she was going to be the prey.

"Have you put my name in this, because... tell me you haven't put my name in this?" Kelly shook the piece of paper that was now crumpled up in her fist at Bethan.

"I haven't," Bethan sighed. "Look, maybe you can just go back to how things were before Emily, but I can't. I have to know why it happened. Because... it's going to happen again, isn't it? The army of dead, the weirdness – that wasn't a blip. Woodsville... it's like a hub, an epicentre... and we have to..."

"Beth, seriously. Give it a rest," Kelly warned her as the table of older girls fell ominously silent, clearly listening in on their conversation.

"But it's not just me. People *are* posting stories – there

are other people out there who know something's going on too," Bethan insisted, shuffling in her chair so that she was directly in Jay's eye-line. Still he managed not to look at her, turning his head automatically in the opposite direction.

Bethan repressed a little sigh. "This girl emailed me about her step-dad. He leaves notes under her pillow, in her drawers, saying he'll always take care of her, always be there for her."

"She should call Social Services." Kelly wrinkled up her nose. "He sounds like a creep."

"He is a creep. A dead creep. He died in a house fire two years ago, fell asleep over beers and a fag, and the whole place went up. It was only luck that this girl and her mum were out at the time. She was glad to see the back of him, but now... well, now he's haunting her."

"He's been leaving her notes for two years?" Kelly's eyebrows shot up. "That is *wrong*."

"No, he's only started haunting her recently. But why now?"

"Maybe he had a hangover." Kelly smirked, winking at Jay. He didn't reply, keeping his gaze trained on the street outside the café, eyes darting from one passing person to the next. Kelly watched him for a moment. After Emily, all of them had changed. Bethan hadn't stopped searching out spooky stories, as if she was trying to put together the kind of puzzle that you could only understand once it was finished. Hashim barely spoke to them, let alone hung out with them. The day after he found Emily's body he'd been back at school, playing footy, giving the teachers hell as if nothing had happened. If anything he was more of a troublemaker than he'd ever been. He'd laugh and joke and bunk off without caring how much detention he got, because he never showed up for it anyway. He'd even started to hang out with some of the kids off the estate, the ones that carried knives and reckoned they were hard. But he wouldn't discuss what happened with Emily. Kelly had tried talking to him and it was impossible. He wouldn't even look her in the eye any more. It was like they had never been friends, like they'd never... well, they'd never started to get close.

Kelly didn't care. She couldn't care less what Hashim and his lame little mates with their stupid penknives got up to. Carter's gang still ruled the estate and everywhere you looked his crew hung out: frustrated angry kids with nothing to do but hate on each other. But since Carter had stopped coming after her, for reasons that Kelly still didn't really understand, she just kept her head down. As far as Hashim was concerned, it was just... well, she'd at least like him to look at her, show her that he remembered that, on that last night, they'd held hands for a bit before everything went pear-shaped. It wasn't her fault that stupid Emily Night went and got herself killed and then didn't remember to behave like a normal dead person. Kelly shuddered.

At least Hashim had gone back to being an exaggerated version of his former self. It was Jay who had changed the most. Normally he'd love the spooky geek fest that Bethan had decided to splash all over the internet. But it was like he was only half-listening to her, like his mind was somewhere else completely – which was weird because Kelly couldn't imagine what else was bigger than the whole "my friend was a ghost and my home town, and probably the world, is on the brink of being taken over by an army of dead people" scenario. Jay looked tired, with purple shadows under his eyes. His face was thin and his skin was so pale that his freckles stood out a mile. He looked like he hadn't slept in weeks. Studying him over her warm, flat imitation cola, Kelly wondered if he saw what she saw when she closed her eyes. The army of dead all around them, pressing forward, whispering threats. Or Emily's mortal remains.

Kelly had only glimpsed what was left of Emily, but that glimpse was enough. Sometimes she'd wake up in the night and just for a split second think she could see Emily sitting on the edge of her bed. But not thin, little, badly-dressed Emily. No, in that split-screamingly-scary second, Kelly would see her corpse, black and twisted, staring with burnt-out eyes.

It was easy to imagine the grey, dirty streets of Woodsville populated by silent, unseen, angry ghosts. When she looked out of the grubby window at the people passing by, heads bent against the freezing wind, ignoring each other as if they were invisible, she wasn't sure it would be that much different.

Just as that thought crossed her mind, Kelly felt a cool hand on the back of her neck, and the fluorescent strip-lighting above her head flickered and dimmed, its monotone buzz stuttering for a moment. Bethan was wittering on, Jay was staring out of the window, the girls sitting behind them were huddled over a plate of chips whispering and giggling. Nothing had changed. Yet Kelly knew someone was standing behind her, touching the back of her neck. And she knew that if she turned round, there would appear to be no one there. But somehow she didn't feel afraid. Instead she felt sort of completed, which sounded stupid, but it was true. For those few seconds she felt safe.

"Kelly, you're not listening." Bethan's insistent voice dragged her back into the conversation. "This girl, Jo Wilcock – we've got to help her, she's really scared..."

"Jo Wilcock?" Kelly hissed, leaning across the table so no one else in the café could hear.

"Yeah, she's in Year Twelve."

"Long hair, pretty face, hangs out with Henry James – that Jo Wilcock?"

Kelly tensed as one of the girls sitting on the next table stifled a giggle with the back of her hand.

"I don't know, I guess so." Bethan looked confused.

"It's a wind-up," Kelly told her, keeping her voice low. "Jo Wilcock hasn't got a dead step-dad. Her step-dad is alive and well, selling second-hand cars at Wilcock's Wheels on City Road."

"Maybe her mum's remarried since the other one burnt to death?" Bethan countered.

Kelly shook her head. "Jo's step-dad has been married to her mum since she was little. Jo's always going on about how he's better than her real dad because he gives her stuff – he's giving her a Mini for her seventeenth."

"But then why would she..." Bethan looked puzzled and hurt. "The email she sent me made her sound really frightened and it's such a horrible story – why would you make that up?"

"Because you are an easy target, Beth," Kelly told her, jerking her head sideways in the direction of their audience. "Look, don't give this lot the laugh they're looking for.

You're already a Goth, you already do your homework on time, and now you're going around telling everyone you believe in ghosts. They've been looking for a new target... don't let them make it you."

"I'm not a Goth—" Bethan began, but Kelly cut her off.

"We know what happened with Emily. But do you really think anyone else wants to believe it, even if half the school saw Emily's ghost themselves? Do you think that one day everyone's going to just stop worrying about who fancies who and go, 'Oh, hang on a minute, there are a truckload of ghosts in this town, we better do something about it'? This blog, it's opening you up to even more grief. You've got blue hair, Beth. Goth or not, that's reason enough for most of the skanks at school to rip you to shreds. You don't need a whacko website to make things worse. Seriously, there's only so much I can do to protect you."

Bethan dropped her head; she knew what Kelly meant. For a while, Kelly had successfully managed to drift between her old group of cool, mean, popular friends, and Bethan and Jay. But that wasn't the natural order of things. Soon enough, the laws of school would demand that balance was restored and Kelly would have to choose between Bethan and Jay or her old life. Hashim had chosen his old life, how long until Kelly did too?

"God, that Jo Wilcock is SO funny," Kelly said suddenly out loud. "Brilliant fake story. You spotted it straightaway, Beth, didn't you?" Kelly stared hard at Bethan.

"Yeah, yeah, well it was a bit obvious," Bethan said unconvincingly. But after a couple more minutes the other girls got up. Kelly was about to breathe a sigh of relief when one of them stopped,

"Were you talking about Jo?" she accused Kelly.

"Yeah," Kelly shrugged. "I'm just saying, she left a really funny prank on Beth's joke blog. It was hysterical, right Beth?"

"It's not a joke blo—"

"So you were talking about her." Wendy raised an eyebrow at Bethan.

"I just said so, didn't I?" Kelly replied.

"Well, don't. Jo doesn't want sad-cases like you even mentioning her name. You want to watch yourself, Kelly. You're losing it."

Kelly twisted her mouth into a tight knot and shrugged. "Whatever."

Bethan waited until the bell on the café door jangled as it shut behind the Year Twelve girls.

"How many of the stories on there do you think are fake then?"

Kelly shook her head. "Probably all of them?"

"Not the Riverbank deaths," Jay said, making the girls jump. They'd almost forgotten he was there. "They're not fake, they're in the paper. And not just the local rag either, nationals too."

"The dead posh girls, you mean?" Kelly yawned. She sprawled over the café table, leaning her chin into her hand. "Everyone who goes to Riverbank is a right stuck-up cow."

"Well, that is one way of looking at it," Jay said. "The other is that four girls from the same school getting horribly, violently killed in the space of a few months is plain weird."

"And if it's weird, then that's where we come in," Bethan added.

"Is it though?" Kelly groaned, burying her face in her hands. "Is it *really*?"

Jay said nothing, his tired eyes relentlessly scanning the busy street outside.

"The press are saying that it's a suicide pact – teenage mass hysteria driving them to it, like that town up north that had twenty teen hangings in the space of six months." Bethan spread a copy of *The Woodsville Gazette* out on the tabletop. The front-page headline read: FOUR FREAK ACCIDENTS LINKED BY TEEN DEATH PACT?

"That's crap." Jay tore his eyes briefly away from the window to look at Bethan. "I mean, if you were going to top yourself you wouldn't *choose* to die the way those girls did."

"Anyway, even if this is something... *Weirdsville*," Kelly grimaced, "how are a bunch of Woodsville comp kids going to get in to Riverbank to find out what's going on? Because, just so you know, my breaking and entering days are over."

"We don't have to break in, we've been invited," Jay told her.

"You what? By who? *Why?*"

"Um... that's kinda my fault," Bethan mumbled. "Since I wrote about Emily on my blog I've had tons of comments, more and more every day. OK, that one from Jo Wilcock was a fake, and maybe some others are too – but they can't all be. I've had *hundreds*, Kel, and not just from kids either, there are loads of people out there who are freaked out."

"By your hair," Kelly teased her.

Bethan rolled her eyes. "And last night I had an email from a girl at Riverbank asking if we would help her."

"You are joking me," Kelly retorted.

Just as Bethan shook her head, a girl with smooth, long blonde hair and bright blue eyes entered the café. Looking over at Bethan, she then made her way to their table.

"Bethan, right? With the blue hair. I'm Charlotte Raimi." She spoke with a soft American accent, quietly as if she were a little shy. "Thank you very much for meeting me. I hope you can help me, I don't know what else to do."

Kelly pressed her lips together and crossed her arms as Charlotte sat down next to her.

"I've tried to get help, but no one takes me seriously. They think I'm making it all up." There was a tremble in Charlotte's voice. "But the girls – my friends that died – it wasn't by accident. They were killed."

"Killed? By who?" Bethan questioned.

"Not by who exactly – more by what," Charlotte said, her fragile composure slipping to reveal an expression of pure fear. "They were cursed, every one of them. Cursed to meet a horrible death and..." Charlotte swallowed, unshed tears glittering in her bright blue eyes, "...and I'm going to be next."

CHAP✝ER TWO

"Why do you think you and the girls that died are cursed?" Jay asked, his green eyes now fixed on Charlotte, Kelly noticed. Honestly, boys were so predictable. Show them a pretty blonde girl in a short skirt and suddenly they were all attentive and interested. She raised an eyebrow, trying to catch Bethan's attention, but Beth blanked her.

"That's a pretty out-there conclusion to jump to," Bethan agreed. Jay's sudden interest hadn't escaped Beth either, but she wanted to know more of Charlotte's story. If it was paranormal, then chances were it would almost certainly have something to do with the mass of ghosts lurking in every corner of Weirdsville. Whenever Bethan looked in a mirror, or switched on a light, she expected to find one staring at her with hollow eyes. She'd developed a sudden newfound aversion to solitude because she knew that the dead were always there. On her way to school, in the bath, shopping in the precinct, even sitting in this café, waiting, waiting – but for what? Death was in every corner, every crack in the pavement, every shadowy doorway, under every bed and behind every wardrobe door.

And the only way Bethan knew how to deal with anything that scared or confused her was to find out as much about it as she could, as if facts could be her armour. She wouldn't stop asking questions until she'd found a way to stop it... because there had to be a way, didn't there? The end of the world wasn't really going to begin in some dead-end new town in the middle of nowhere, was it?

"Go on," Kelly said. "Explain."

Charlotte thought for a moment, biting her lip and twisting her fingers into knots.

"It's boring up at school, you know, a hundred girls – nothing to do. We're not allowed to come into town—"

"In case you're mugged by chavs?" Kelly interrupted.

"Partly," Charlotte admitted, eyeing Kelly up and down and then putting her hand over her mobile and drawing it closer. "But also it's school policy to be extra... strict. Our parents pay to make sure we don't do anything fun. No decent TV, no music except at weekends, and certainly no boys." She treated Jay to a sideways look that made the tips of his ears go pink.

"I heard it was harsh up there," Bethan said. "But that sounds like prison."

"Yeah, I thought girls' schools were all midnight feasts and jolly hockey sticks," Kelly joked, putting on a posh accent. Charlotte ignored her.

"That's exactly what Riverbank is, a prison for wayward girls."

"You're a wayward girl?" Jay sounded impressed. "I've always wanted to meet one of those."

Charlotte giggled, her frightened, tense expression vanishing completely for a few seconds as she smiled. "My parents live in Boston. I've been kicked out of more schools within a thousand-mile radius than they can find to send me to," she told them. "They heard about Riverbank from a client of my dad. This guy's third wife had something to do with arson and grand theft auto when she was a teen. Riverbank turned her into a *lady*. So here I am, in wet, grey, hideous Woodsville – not even near anywhere good, like London or Manchester!"

Kelly scowled. Woodsville may be a disgusting, crime-ridden, apocalyptic dump, but she didn't take kindly to an outsider slagging it off.

"Mum and Dad couldn't wait to see the back of me; the further away they could send me, the better. There are other girls from overseas too, and some British kids – basically, we're the ones who have parents rich enough to keep us out of juvenile detention."

"And you look like a lady too," Jay said. All three girls looked at him. "I just said that out loud, didn't I?" He cringed, burying his pink face in his long fingers.

"So what's the worst thing you've done?" Kelly asked her. "Forgot to wear a hat in church?"

Charlotte raised a beautifully shaped eyebrow. "Riverbank girls don't dwell on the past, we focus on the future."

"So, broken a nail and shoplifted a lipstick then?" Kelly countered. "I bet I've done a lot worse than you."

"I bet you have," Charlotte retorted. "But that's the difference between us. In your case, it doesn't matter."

Bethan stepped in. "Kelly, it's not about what Charlotte's done in the past. What matters is why Charlotte thinks she is cursed and why four of her friends are dead."

Charlotte's demeanour changed as Bethan spoke, her shoulders sinking, her hands knotting as if she'd only just remembered why she was there.

Kelly bristled, but said nothing. One thing she had reluctantly learnt recently was that you couldn't judge a book by its cover. Stupid, skinny Emily Night had turned out to be brave and loyal, if a bit dead. Besides, when people looked at Kelly they usually didn't see past her hooped earrings, discount clothes and attitude... So maybe this Charlotte was all right. It would be a struggle, but Kelly decided not to hate her straightaway. At least, not until she had a good reason to.

"As I've told you, life at Riverbank is deathly dull, and so we make up stuff to do. The school is a real old building, a manor house dating back from before the English Civil War. It's got these big attics, full of junk left over going years back. We go up there after lights-out sometimes, to talk and smoke, drink a little, listen to music – you know."

Bethan nodded knowingly, although her nearest experience to smoking had been accidentally inhaling cigarette smoke at a bus stop, which had made her gag and cough for nearly ten minutes and vow never to light one herself. The only time she'd ever drunk anything alcoholic she'd been sick for three days straight.

"So we're up there one night, and we find this trunk of stuff. Clothes, not uniforms, but girls' things, like from the olden days, and we're trying them on for a laugh when at the bottom, underneath a load of old rubbish, Tara..."

Charlotte paused, her confident tone fading. "Tara, my best friend at Riverbank, pulled out a Ouija board."

"A wee-ja-what?" Kelly asked. "Sounds unhygienic to me."

"No, a Ouija board," Jay explained. "Spelt O.U.I.J.A. It's supposed to derive from the French and Dutch for 'yes', you know. Because of the yes-no responses asked of spirits in a séance situation."

"Huh?" Kelly looked confused.

"Have you never seen *The Exorcist*?" Jay asked her, shaking his head.

"Is it on MTV?" Kelly retorted.

Jay sighed. "It's like a board with the letters of the alphabet round the outside and the words 'yes' and 'no' printed on it. It comes with a planchette – a big counter to rest on the board that spirits move around, pointing at letters to spell out messages. You supposedly use it to communicate with the dead, however many people believe that the planchette is moved by ideomotor action – which means that although you might think it's a ghost moving the counter, it's actually the power of your own subconscious thought."

The three girls stared at him.

"Is he always like this?" Charlotte asked.

"Afraid so," Bethan admitted.

"Geektastic," Kelly added.

"Normally I'd be running a mile, but it's so long since I've seen any boys that I'm thinking he's actually kind of cute." One corner of Charlotte's mouth curled into a smile and even Kelly couldn't help smirking as she watched Jay go bright red. *Hashim would love Charlotte*, she thought, suddenly missing him with a sharp pang. He'd think she was funny and pretty, and he'd flirt with her like Jay didn't know how to. Kelly's smile faded, maybe it was just as well Hashim wasn't here.

"I don't know about subconscious thought," Charlotte went on. "But there were five of us up there that night..." Her expression shifted again like a sudden breeze rippling the surface of calm water, and fear crept back into her eyes. "We were messing around, you know, lit a few candles, turned out the lights. One minute we were just giggling, laughing, asking who would be the next to get a boyfriend, who had the fattest thighs..."

"The usual sort of thing you talk over with the dead," Kelly mumbled. "Cos they like nothing more than to discuss negative body-image issues in the afterlife."

"And then the next minute everything changed," Charlotte talked over her. "It was like the dark got... thicker, heavier.

There was just this little pool of light from the candles with us sitting in it, and I got the strangest feeling that if we stepped even a millimetre out of the light or if it went out, that something really, really bad would happen. It felt like we weren't alone any more. I *had* been pushing the counter around before; just like the others – but then suddenly it was moving on its own. I felt it sliding along under my fingers and I couldn't stop it. It felt like the tips of my fingers were dipped in ice water."

Charlotte paused. The clock on the greasy café wall stopped ticking and the radio on the shelf that had been blaring out generic R&B suddenly switched to static. It was as if the whole room was listening.

"What question did you ask just before this happened?" Bethan asked, scribbling furiously in her notebook, her voice sounding way too loud in the hushed room.

Charlotte dragged her fingers through her hair, and Kelly noticed that the tips of her painted nails were ragged, the varnish worn away by chewing. "We'd asked which one of us would die first. And it was like the temperature dropped in a split second. Around us the whole room, the boxes of junk and old furniture, started to vibrate and rattle. We were so scared. We took our hands off the board, but the arrow..." Charlotte swallowed, staring at the tabletop as if she could still see the Ouija board. "It kept moving, real quick, sliding from one letter to the next, faster and faster. It pointed at T.A.R.A. then L.U.C.Y., then D.E.N.I.S.E., then J.A.D.E. and finally me. It spelt out a message, so fast it was hard to keep up. Then we got it..."

"Was it 'Jeggings are out'?" Kelly snapped. She knew she was being flippant, but she was desperate to break the ominous oppressive tension that had built up. The sun had dropped below the skyline whilst they had been talking and the street light outside had briefly flickered on then sputtered out. The pavement that had been busy with people coming home from school and work was all but deserted, except for a couple of commuters standing at the bus stop across the road. As Kelly stared at the figures, huddled against the cold, their edges seemed to blur and fade into the thick shadows behind them, leaving the bus shelter eerily empty, except for a ragged-looking pigeon.

"What was the message?" Jay shifted in his seat, looking uncomfortable.

There was a long silence and then all of them jumped as the radio came briefly back to life and a man's voice blared out "Get out, get away now!" before it started crackling with white noise again. The weary café owner bashed it with a broom handle, and the rhythmic repetition of R&B blared out once again.

"All here cursed with death," Charlotte whispered, closing her eyes for a moment and taking a breath. "That's what the message said. And then, in a heartbeat, everything changed again; the shadows went, the room warmed up and it seemed like the mouldy old attic we always hung out in. But when we switched the light back on and looked around, everything was messed up. Chairs had been turned upside down, wardrobes and massive old trunks thrown around as if they were made of paper. There was junk everywhere and it took us ages to move the trunk that we'd found the board in from the top of the stairs – it was blocking our way down."

"All of that must have made quite a racket. Didn't anyone hear and come up to find out what was going on?" Jay asked her.

Charlotte shook her head. "It was like it happened in an instant and in silence. When we got back to our dorm we freaked out. We were afraid to close our eyes, in case we didn't wake up... But then the next day it was sunny, we had double maths and none of what happened seemed real any more. We were laughing about it by lunchtime, convincing ourselves it was all in our hysterical little heads – do you know what I mean?"

Bethan, Jay and Kelly exchanged a look. They knew all about denial; they were fast becoming experts on the subject.

"About a week went by. We didn't go back up to the attic, and things were back to normal. Everything seemed like a distant dream, or a film.

"Then Tara died, I mean, she was killed. I guess you know how."

"It was in the paper." Bethan nodded. The fifteen-year-old girl's death had been described in glorious gory detail in the *Woodsville Gazette* Bethan had brought with her. When Bethan had read about it at first she was shocked and horrified, and then she realised rather ashamedly, sort of fascinated. She couldn't stop imagining what it must have been like for Tara to die that way knowing there was nothing she could do to save herself, and how much it must have hurt.

What it must feel like to die was something that Bethan had once found hard to understand, but recently she thought about very little else. Once she had felt immortal, but now it seemed to her that there wasn't much keeping her on the right side of life, one missed step, one wrong turn...

Charlotte continued, "Tara wasn't herself that day. We thought she was just getting her period or something. She was irrational, angry. But if we'd have stuck with her, then maybe it wouldn't have happened..." Charlotte trailed off.

"What did happen?" Kelly asked. "The last time I saw a newspaper it was wrapped round some chips."

"Really? You do surprise me," Charlotte replied instantly, obviously fluent in bitch.

Bethan and Jay exchanged uncomfortable glances, but Charlotte squared up her shoulders and began to talk.

"It was garbage day. There are these great big dumpsters out the back of the school for all the trash. Tara woke up in a panic. She couldn't find this little necklace her boyfriend had given her. It was a piece of junk and I'm pretty sure he'd dumped her because she hadn't heard from him in weeks – she never liked him that much anyway – but suddenly she was obsessed with finding it. The last thing she said to me was that she was skipping breakfast to go look for it."

"Then what?" Bethan asked, scribbling 'lost necklace' into her notebook followed by 'necklace curse? How? Why?' She caught Kelly reading over her shoulder and covered her words with her hand.

"Tara didn't turn up to class, but that was nothing new. I covered for her, said she was in bed, sick, to buy her a bit more time. We guessed she was still looking for that stupid necklace. Lunchtime came and went and we still hadn't seen her." Charlotte dipped her head. "I remember seeing the police car coming up the drive. As soon as I saw it, I knew."

Charlotte sniffed, rubbing the back of her hand across her eyes. "Look, if you want the gory stuff, read the papers. Tara must have fallen into a dumpster looking for that stupid necklace and knocked herself out. When the truck arrived and collected the rubbish, they didn't notice her. She was crushed to death. But the really awful thing that I can't get out of my head is that she knew what was happening. The police said she must've woken up in the truck. All of her fingernails were broken and torn where she'd tried to claw her way out."

"Oh my God," Kelly said. "That is... rank."

"The arrow, planchette, whatever you call it... pointed to Tara first. Then Lucy, and she was killed a few weeks after. Denise was about a month later and then a few weeks ago, Jade. Now... now there's only me."

The café owner coughed loudly, phlegm rattling in his chest. "I'm closing up, kids," he wheezed. "Don't stay open past six any more, can't afford to keep replacing the glass. I've got to get the grates on, so finish up, OK?"

"We'll just be a sec," Kelly told him.

"Won't mind if I clean the floor around you then, will you?" He smiled a gappy, rotten-toothed smile. "To be honest, I like the company. Last bloke to own this place died in a chip-pan accident. Slipped on some oil on the floor or something; they found him head in the fryer, all his face burnt off, what was left covered in batter. Sometimes I get the feeling he hasn't quite moved out yet, like he's still here looking over my shoulder," the café owner chuckled to himself.

"Nice," Kelly said, making a face.

"So," Bethan said, keeping one eye on the café owner as he lumbered around with his broom. "They were talking about the whole mass hysteria thing on the news last night. A couple of years ago at a school in Ireland one of the pupils had a massive epileptic fit and died. The others were so surprised and upset that someone their age, who they knew, could just drop down dead that a wave of hysteria swept through the school. There were mass faintings, fits – even an attempted overdose. Girls were running through the corridors screaming. Do you think that might be what's happened at Riverbank?"

Charlotte shook her head impatiently. "Riverbank girls are the sort who cause mass hysteria, not get it. At her last school, Tara released African bird-eating spiders into the girls' locker room. Apparently you could hear the screams for miles around. She wasn't the sort to get easily spooked, and anyway, even if she was, how would that cause four deaths?"

"Mass hysteria is a powerful thing," Jay said thoughtfully. "There have been many documented cases of it sweeping through whole towns; even cities. In Halifax in the thirties, there was a full-scale panic because of a rumour about a madman stalking the streets with a knife, attacking innocent women. Shops shut, businesses closed, no one dared go out. People were reporting they'd been attacked, some with serious wounds. Only there was no madman, there never had been – it *was* just a rumour. Some people had actually stabbed themselves. It happens."

"Hurt themselves maybe... but not killed themselves, and not how Tara died," Charlotte insisted. "Ofsted have closed the school down for an independent inquiry. They've sent most of the kids and staff home so there's just a few of us left, with a couple of teachers. Riverbank gets bigger and emptier and scarier every day, and I can feel whatever it is, waiting for me. And I know that if I don't do something, I will be next. I'm sixteen. I don't want to die. Please... help me."

Jay looked at his friends. In their own way, they each knew exactly how that felt.

"Look, Charlotte, the thing is, I don't even know if we can help you. We're not experts, we just got involved by accident with something that none of us can explain. And what happened to us, it's so different from what happened to you..." Jay dropped his gaze.

"But there is something we can do," Bethan cut in. "When Emily first told us about the ghosts, we set out to prove that what she thought was happening wasn't real."

"Yeah, but it was real; really real," Kelly reminded her.

"So why don't we do the same thing? Why don't we find this board and do another séance to see if it's real?"

"No." Charlotte shook her head. "No way. I'm never going near that thing again."

"But Bethan's right. That really is pretty much the only thing we can do at this stage," Jay told her. "I'm sorry, Charlotte."

Charlotte looked thoughtful as the café owner washed the floor with grey-coloured water, humming a completely different tune to the one on the radio.

"I don't know what else to do," she shrugged, pushing a piece of paper across the table. "This is my number. I've got to get back. School might be more or less closed, but they'll still kill me before the curse does if they catch me out of bounds. Text me later, I'll work out when to let you in."

"OK," Jay said staring at the piece of paper, like he'd never seen a girl's phone number before.

"Charlotte, this is going to sound a bit odd," Bethan said rather awkwardly as the other girl got up. "But... um... you're sure you're not already dead, aren't you?"

CHAPTER THREE

*J*ay spent the walk home listening to Kelly and Bethan discuss Charlotte in every tiny detail. Kelly complained that she'd obviously spent at least half an hour straightening her hair, even though she was supposed to be terrified to death. Her shoes were too high, her skirt was too short and her mascara was too obvious.

"What if she's a fake too? What if she's some flipping am-dram fake, trying to wind us up like Jo?" Kelly said. "Didn't you notice, one minute she was in tears and shaking and then the next she was Little Miss Perfect."

"It was probably just a front," Bethan said. "I mean, some people put on a front to hide how they are really feeling, don't they, Kel?"

Girls are funny, Jay thought, letting their chatter fade

into the background. They always went on about how they stick together and that the world would be a better place if they were in charge, but when it came down to it, he wasn't that sure that any of them really liked each other at all. Not even Bethan and Kelly sometimes.

He'd liked Charlotte. Yes, for all the reasons that Kelly didn't, and because she'd flirted, not with him exactly, but at him, even though she was scared out of her wits. Jay was pretty certain that Charlotte would be a lot of fun to hang out with under more normal circumstances. The kind of girl who would get you into all sorts of trouble and crush you like a fly if you got on her nerves, but fun. Problem was, the world was not a normal place. Especially not since the day Jay had turned a corner and bumped into himself.

He'd stood there staring, not at another person who looked a lot like him, but at *himself*. And his other self had said to come with him, because if he did there was still a chance that people he cared about might not die.

Jay had looked into his own eyes and seen the fake bravado there, the attempt to try and keep calm. His heart pounded, his head felt like it might explode, adrenalin pumped through his veins. It was fight or flight, and in a split second he had taken the second option, running away as fast as he could. And as he ran with his lungs burning and his legs shaking, he had the oddest sensation that a little piece of him was still stuck like gum to the pavement. That he was being torn in two, leaving some vital part of him behind, glued to the spot where his double had stood.

Running had been a gut reaction and he'd regretted it ever since. Now it felt like he was caught in a sort of suspended animation, simultaneously terrified of both seeing and never seeing himself again; afraid of not knowing what it meant to meet himself and frightened of finding out. What were you supposed to do when the impossible happened? Since that morning, he'd felt hollow and he kept waking up in the middle of the night panicking about losing something important. Jay tried his best to be rational, to think things through like a scientist, but no matter how hard he tried Jay couldn't shake the feeling that he had somehow lost his soul. And there was one other thing that Jay hadn't the courage to think about until he was back at home, his bedroom door slammed and bolted behind him and his duvet dragged over his head.

The hands and clothes of the other version of him had been covered in black sticky stuff that smelt tinny – sharp and metallic. It had been blood. Dried sticky blood.

It wasn't until Kelly called his name that Jay realised that he'd stopped walking and was stood stock-still in the middle of the estate, the four tower blocks seeming to bend and peer down at him, an insignificant speck of life lost in all the concrete.

"Jay, you coming?" Kelly asked him impatiently.

He'd been putting it off, but Jay knew that there was only one person he could talk to about what had happened to him. That one person also happened to be very old and quite possibly mad, but at least he would take Jay seriously. He had to go and see Albert, his grandad – if anyone knew what it meant to meet yourself, then Albert would. It couldn't be put off any longer – especially if he had somehow put his friends in danger.

"I've got to go see Grandad," Jay said, nodding at the tower in which Albert lived on the top floor.

"Oh, shall we come?" Bethan offered, brandishing her ring-binder. "If you're going to ask him about Ouija boards, I could take notes."

Jay shook his head. "No... I've got to do something for my mum. I'll ask him what he knows while I'm there, OK?"

"Sure?" Kelly asked, studying his face with her cool grey eyes.

"Sure." Jay broke her gaze and examined the pavement, studded with the flat grey discs of discarded gum.

"Well, if you say so." Kelly shrugged and turned on her heel, linking her arm through Bethan's. "If you hear from Charlotte, let us know. Don't go meeting her on your own, OK? Never mind protecting her from curses. You need us to protect you from her."

As Jay approached the entrance to the tower he noticed that someone had broken the protective metal cage that shielded the outside light, and then smashed the bulb, leaving the covered porch shadowy and dark, safe from the prying eyes of CCTV. He was quite close by the time he realised that there were several people blocking the door: some older kids and a younger one on a bike, probably a delivery boy for some dealer. They always used minors to handle drop-offs, because if they got nicked nothing much happened to them. Jay hesitated. He didn't recognise any of them, not even by sight. Maybe if he ignored them, they'd leave him alone.

As he walked towards the group a large boy in a dark hoody, holding a small squat dog on a chain, peered at him. His sharp features flared into relief as another kid lit up. Taking a deep breath, Jay did his best to saunter casually towards the door, although acting was never really his strong point, even at the best of times.

The big kid with the dog barred his way.

"Scuse," Jay said amiably, nodding at the door. The kid didn't move.

"Scuse, please," Jay said again, hoping the magic word might help.

"Where you going, ginger?" the kid asked him.

"To visit my... girl." Jay lied at the last minute, sensing a trip to grandparents wouldn't quite cut it.

"Hooking up, yeah? Nice one." The kid grinned at his mates, who shuffled, coughed and sniffed but didn't seem to talk. "You know what, you should take her something. Got any cash on you?"

He flicked out his hand and between his fingers was a little baggie. Jay couldn't see what was in it in the dark, but knew it would be some kind of drug.

"No, man, I'm skint and anyway, I don't—" Jay began.

"It's cool, it's cool." The boy clapped a heavy hand on his shoulder, at the same time stuffing the baggie into Jay's jacket pocket. "Pay me next time."

"Really, I don't want anything..." But the kid had already stepped out of the way, opening the door and showing Jay through it like a very gracious host.

"I said, payment next time, bruv."

The sight of the open door was such a relief that Jay made his way through without any further protest.

"Don't worry about finding me, yeah? I'll find you when I want you. No worries."

Once safely in the lift, Jay took the baggie out of his pocket. It contained a small amount of white powder, probably speed – cheap and easy to come by on the estate, mainly because it was cut with sherbet if you were lucky and scouring powder if you weren't. Unsure of what to do with it, Jay stuffed the baggie back into his pocket. For now he had more important things to worry about.

Albert didn't talk for a long time after Jay had described bumping into himself. Jay was used to that; Grandad liked to think things over, as if he were going through all of the things he had stored in his head until he found the right fact. Jay watched him, head bowed, rubbing his good eye with the arthritic fingers of one hand whilst the other drummed on the arm of his wheelchair. Suddenly he looked lost and old. No longer like the piratical, slightly mad old man who still seemed capable of taking on the world, even though he wore an eyepatch and had had both of his legs amputated several years before.

"This is what I was thinking," Jay spoke, unable to bear the silence any more. "Maybe it was, like, just shock. After everything with Emily – finding out I'd been hanging out with a dead person – that could make a lot of people go a bit ga-ga. On the day when I saw it, him... me, I hadn't slept for two days. When you're tired, you hallucinate, don't you?"

"Did it feel like a dream, as if you were sleepwalking?" Albert asked him. Reluctantly, Jay shook his head.

"No, no... it felt very, very real. Hyper-real. You know that if you're in an accident, like a car crash or something, everything slows right down because your brain is giving you time to react? Well, it felt like that. And I reacted by running away."

Jay waited, but Albert didn't speak again. He just kept shaking his head as if he'd been given some very bad news.

"OK... so then I'm thinking parallel universe. We already know that there has to be intelligent life out there, and that there is something other than the universe in space, because the universe is expanding, right? So it has to be expanding into something... Well, many astrophysicists think that it's perfectly likely that there are thousands, millions of parallel universes existing in the same space. If that's so, and if time and space is something that can be bent or opened up, like through a black hole or something, then maybe there is *another Jay*, in another universe and he somehow made it through to this one. He wanted to tell me about... something that was going to happen, that he somehow found out about in this universe, because maybe..." Jay trailed off. He'd succeeded in confusing himself.

"I read that if something happens to you – say you are run over by a bus – then a new universe is instantly created. *One where you live on*. In the old universe you are dead, but in the new one you have a near miss, avoid the bus and carry on living. So maybe, maybe the me that I saw is from another universe, one where I got hit by a bus, and he has found a portal from that universe to this one to... warn me to stay away from buses?"

Albert shook his head. "Stay away from buses," he muttered.

Jay's stomach churned, he'd never seen his grandad look so sad and it frightened him. When Albert finally looked up, a tear was rolling from his good eye.

"What you call parallel universes, I call the fourth dimension – heaven maybe or even hell – yes, it exists. That's where the dead are supposed to go. Most of them get there through the gaps in the warp and weft of time. And once you're there, you stay there. You're not supposed to come back again. But here in Woodsville there's little warp and weft: it's tightly woven. Ghosts don't go when they should, you see, and then they don't want anyone else to get through either. It's been happening for years, ever since I was a young man..." Albert shook his head. "The thing is, son, you can't get through in a spaceship or a black-hole thingy. Even if you came across a so-called portal, you couldn't go through it. Your physical body won't let you. There are only two ways to visit another dimension: astral projection and death."

"But I'm not dead!" Jay exclaimed, patting his torso as proof.

"Son," Albert said, his tone grave. "You don't have to be dead to see your own ghost." Jay stared at him, his heart contracting as he suddenly realised exactly how frightened his grandad was.

"What do you mean?" Jay's voice was croaky, his throat bone dry.

"Ghost omens, Jay. A death, a warning, an omen," Albert said. "Every culture has its legend of someone meeting their Doppelganger, and in every case it's a foretelling of death. The poet Shelley met himself just before he drowned, and Abraham Lincoln saw his double standing behind him in a mirror on the eve of his assassination."

Unable to look his grandad in the face any more, Jay looked around Albert's tiny cluttered flat, piles of paper stacked almost ceiling-high. It hadn't been decorated since long before Jay was born and bright garish wallpaper exploded in the few uncovered patches of wall. It was the flat of a dear but very old man who told a lot of stories and often made little or no sense. Sometimes Albert liked to act a bit mad, sometimes he was a bit mad. Jay had never really been able to tell the difference, but it had never really mattered before. He looked at the shelf of his granny's figurines, still taking pride of place over the telly, tiny china cats in ballet dresses, a thick film of dust coating their heads. This was a warm, happy, safe place, where Jay had always loved to come since he was very little. And now his grandad was talking about omens, warnings, death. None of it seemed real.

"Ghosts can travel back and forth through time. They can see the future, as well as relive the past. Ghost omens go back to warn their living selves that something terrible is coming. That death is coming. Son, a ghost omen... it means you are..." Albert's mouth worked, but for several moments no sound came out. When it did, it was barely more than a whisper. "It means you are going to die."

"No! I mean, no, that's stupid," Jay said edgily. "He said... I said that there was a chance I could save everyone's life. That if I went with him, there'd be a chance I might not die. Say you are right, say it was a ghost omen – well, then that's the *whole point* of a warning. It gives you a chance to be saved!"

Albert kept shaking his head. "There has never been a ghost omen that has prevented its own death. Once you are dead, you are dead, Jay. If death has happened in the past or the present or the future, you can't undo it. It's already done. Maybe your ghost didn't know that or maybe... maybe he was hoping he wouldn't have to tell you."

Jay stood up abruptly, knocking the chair he'd been sitting on, on to its back.

"No, Grandad – you've got to be wrong! He was covered in blood, dried sticky blood, lots of it, like he'd been injured really badly. I don't want... I don't want that to happen to me."

Albert stretched out a trembling hand towards Jay pacing across the carpet, but he couldn't reach him.

"I ran away, Grandad, I ran away. He was going to tell me the most important thing anyone will ever tell me and I ran away. I'm not even sixteen yet," Jay said, thinking how he'd barely listened to Charlotte when she'd said virtually the same thing. "What if I find him and ask him what's going to happen? Then I'll just be able to avoid whatever it is..."

Albert stared at Jay for a moment longer, tears standing in his eye. "Omen means death," he said slowly, carefully. "Always death."

Jay stopped pacing and looked at him. "How do you know? You don't know everything, you know!" he all but shouted.

"No, I don't." Albert pinched his thumb and forefinger over the bridge of his nose.

"It's like when you only ever get to see bad news on TV, never the good stuff. What is the point of a warning, if there's nothing you can do about it?" Jay said, his eyes bright and cheeks flushed. "I have to find him, and ask him what to do to stop anyone dying, including me."

Albert closed his eyes and the flat drifted into silence, except for the creaking of the radiators and the drip, drip, drip of the kitchen tap. "Perhaps... you'll need your friend, the destroyer of evil. Ghosts swarm round him like bees to honey."

"Hashim?" With his racing heart slowing gradually, Jay righted the chair and sank into it. Suddenly he felt really tired, as if in those last five minutes he'd lived five years of his life all at once. "I'm not sure, since Emily he's stayed away."

"He'll come back. He hasn't got any choice, not if—" Albert stopped himself.

"What?" Jay pressed him.

"Hashim's the only thing we've got standing between us and who knows what."

Albert picked up the salt-cellar and tipped it up so that a steady flow of salt quickly built into a mountain on the tabletop.

"Salt guards against evil," he muttered.

"Well, Hashim's too busy playing footy and messing around with girls." Jay got up, fighting the wave of tears that threatened to entirely dissolve him. "I guess I'll have to find my own ghost."

"Jay!" Albert said as his grandson picked up his jacket. "Jay!"

"What?" Jay sobbed, unable to look at him.

Albert held out his arms. "Come here, son, give your old grandad a hug."

Jay paused, then kneeling on the cold kitchen floor put his arms around his grandad, inhaling the scent of stale cigarettes and beer.

"You know I love you more than anyone. I'd die in your place, Jay, in a minute. The thought of me being stuck here, in this chair, without you..."

"Don't let it happen, Grandad, promise?" Jay begged, all too aware that he sounded about five years old and wishing that he was.

"Promise," Albert whispered into his hair.

Jay studied his grandfather's lined and creviced face,

battered and scarred by life. There was so much that he wanted to say, so much he needed to hear. He could see the strain in Albert's expression and for a moment it felt like they were the only two people left alive in this dark, deathly town, surrounded by the dead. "And if I see him... I mean, me again?"

"Then whatever you do, don't run."

CHAP✝ER FOUR

Kelly pressed her palm against her bedroom window as hard as she could, until the chill of the glass beneath her skin warmed to her blood and she felt her skin cool and numb. When she took her hand away, a ghostly impression of it was left imprinted on the glass and the bumps and ridges of her hand were flat and white, making it look like a negative of an old photo.

Once, a couple of years ago, after her dad had gone out on Friday night and still hadn't come back by Tuesday, Kelly had dragged up the courage to go into his room. Both she and her brother, Sean, had been warned to never go in there, at the risk of a beating, and even though Kelly had suffered as much for breaking a mug or leaving her hair in the sink, she obeyed this rule. She got the feeling that the punishment for breaking it would be much worse than any she'd suffered before.

Sean had been in the front room on the PlayStation. Kelly knew that nothing was going to tear him away from *Need for Speed*, so she pushed open her dad's bedroom door, his grubby fingerprints smeared on the once-white gloss paint like a final warning of what would happen if she was caught.

Kelly wasn't looking for the six or seven PCs that were piled up in a haphazard tower in the corner of the room, or the sandwich bag full of a confetti of credit cards that glittered on her dad's bed. Kelly's dad didn't have a job, but you couldn't say he didn't work. He wheeled and dealed in the backroom of The Slaughtered Lamb from the minute it opened to the minute it closed, and then staggered home, his mood determined by how well he'd done that day.

Despite the risk, Kelly was looking for something, anything that would tell her about her mother. She'd left when Kelly was only small, barely more than a baby. Although Kelly told herself that she couldn't care less about a woman who obviously didn't care about her, there was always something nagging at the edges of her memory, like a tiny splinter, dug in deep, infected, niggling away. When Kelly thought about her mum, this feeling of unease and anxiety washed over her, making her shudder, like someone was walking over her grave. Kelly didn't remember much about her mum, but if she could find something, some clue to what kind of person she had been or why she'd left her two young children behind, then maybe the feeling would go away.

Her dad's room stank of stale ashtrays, unwashed sheets and clothes. There were piles and piles of junk, stuffed into carrier bags everywhere she looked. The curtains, made of thin blue nylon, were permanently drawn and the window was always left open a crack. They'd fluttered against the afternoon breeze, letting triangles of daylight in every now and then, darting across the bed.

Kelly had no idea where to start. She'd looked at the wardrobe, doors open on an assortment of fake designer tracksuits, labels still attached, spilling out on to the carpet. If she'd gone in there, he'd know. And he kept the drawers locked. Kelly had hesitated, her hand on the door handle. He'll be back, she'd thought – any minute he could be back and then... She winced from memory. It was too risky.

But just as she had been about to turn back a large gust of wind blew hard through the window, turning the intermittent chinks of light into a beam, and it was then that Kelly saw the corner of something, a shoebox maybe, peeking out under the edge of the duvet. Glancing over her shoulder,

Kelly pushed the door shut and, kneeling on the dusty carpet, pulled the box out. It was an old shoebox, not for trainers, or men's shoes, but for a pair of women's heels. Kelly had looked at the illustration of the shoes that had once occupied the box, on a label that was still stuck to one end. They were high and strappy with an open toe. The description under the drawing read: Cassandra, POPPY RED.

They could just have been something else that her dad had picked up off the back of a van, but somehow, as Kelly stroked the thick dust from the box's lid she felt that it had to be her mother's box, that they'd been her mother's shoes. They were fun and carefree shoes; the shoes of a woman who loved to dance. For a split second, Kelly imagined her mother creeping out of the flat in the dead of night in her red high heels.

Breathless, she'd carefully lifted the lid off, praying that she would find something inside; letters maybe or photos. Her heart had sunk when she realised that the box was empty. There was nothing in it except some crumpled and crumbly tissue paper, that Kelly guessed had once padded out the toes of those strappy sandals. Dismayed she picked the box up and tipped it up. Out fluttered something: thin strips of dark see-through plastic. When Kelly picked one up she could see that the strip had some sort of pattern on it. She held it up to the light and gasped. As the sun shone through there was a ghostly image of a woman, with her arm around a child and a baby on her lap. All the parts of her that should have been dark were stark white, like the shadows under her eyes and her hair. And all the parts of her that should have been light were dark, like her black-toothed open smile. It was the negative of an old-fashioned photo. On a sharp inward breath Kelly realised she could be looking at an image of her mother.

Quickly she'd gathered up the other slips of film and held them, one by one, up to the light, staring and staring at each image in turn. Her mother had been born in Jamaica and Kelly remembered, or thought she did, how her soft, smooth, rich-brown skin would seem to glow from the inside out on a sunny day, like the sunshine was somehow trapped within. And in Kelly's memory her dark eyes would flash when she laughed. Did she remember that or did she dream it?

Then it dawned on Kelly. She could take these negatives to the photographic shop on the precinct, the one with the pictures of brides and grooms and babies and kittens in the window, and ask them to turn them into photos. She could have all of these pictures of her mum.

Then the front door had slammed and her father bellowed, "Kelly, get the kettle on and make me some dinner, I'm bloody starving!" Kelly froze, clutching the negatives in her palm. "Where is the silly cow?"

She heard her father lurch into the living room, swearing loudly.

"You waste of space!" he'd yelled at her brother. Kelly didn't know what happened after that, but she guessed he'd ripped the controller from Sean's hand and thrown it because she heard a crash and then shouting. Her brother had grown pretty big by those days so Dad mostly left him alone. Kelly knew they wouldn't be arguing for long.

Quickly she'd put the lid back on the box, hesitating when she saw the streaks her fingers had left in the dust, and then pushed it back under the bed, stuffing the strips of negatives into her pocket and opening the door.

She came face to face with her dad.

"What do you think you're doing?" he'd asked her. His voice was low, thick and smelt of beer. He braced his arms against the doorframe, barring her exit.

"I heard something," Kelly said, smiling at her dad. "I heard scrabbling around and you know, her next-door, well I saw her in the lift on the way back from school and she said she had rats. And I heard the noise in your room, so I just went in, just for a second, to make sure there weren't any rats."

"Rats on the twentieth floor?" Dad leant in closer. "What

you got in your pocket, Kelly? If you've been in my stuff, I'll—"

Kelly tried to duck under his arm, but he grabbed her wrist, twisting it as he jerked her backwards, slamming her spine against the doorframe.

"I haven't, I haven't been in your stuff, Dad, I haven't," she'd sobbed. "I was just looking, I just..." Kelly hated how pathetic she'd been, caving in to put off his anger for a few seconds more. She'd pulled the now crumpled strips from her pocket and showed them to him.

"I found these... Are they photos of Mum?" Kelly had asked hesitantly.

"Are they photos of...? You silly little cow." Viciously Kelly's dad hauled her by the wrist into the kitchen, grabbing the negatives and dropping them into the sink which was piled high with dirty dishes. "You want to see a picture of your mummy, do you? Your mummy who left you without a second glance and who has never been back, or called or even sent you a birthday card since. You want a photo of her, do you?"

"I just... I just thought..." Kelly sobbed as her dad put his hand on the back of her neck and pushed her face over the sink.

"You don't think, Kelly," he'd said. Then he reached under the sink and took a bottle out, Kelly wasn't sure what was in it but it stank and burnt the inside of her nostrils, as he poured it over the dishes and negatives at once.

"You want to see a photo of your mum, do you?" He'd laughed and with one flick of his lighter, set fire to the negatives. The flames whooshed up, making Kelly jerk back but her dad held her there as the delicate strips quickly blackened and curled, flakes of ash wafting upward and turning to dust.

Kelly had watched, wondering if this was her last chance to ever see her mother's face. The next thing she knew, she was sprawled on the kitchen floor, pain shooting through her jaw, blood on her lips.

"I told you, don't go in my room." Her dad leant over her and Kelly braced herself for more.

"You stupid old man," she heard Sean say. "You want a fight, fight me, you coward." Kelly shrank back in the corner as her brother pushed their dad hard against the sink. She caught Sean's look, which told her: *run*. And so she did, out of the front door, without a coat. Kelly didn't go back until long after dark when she knew Dad would have either gone out or passed out.

When she'd pushed open his bedroom door, Sean had been asleep, lying curled up on his bed. Gently, Kelly touched his shoulder and he flinched, turning over. One side of his face was broken and bruised, but he grinned when he saw her.

"I went looking for you. Where'd you get to? You shouldn't be hanging around out there on your own."

"What could happen that's worse than here?" Kelly whispered.

"You should see him, Kel," Sean winced as he sat up. "He knows he can't walk over me, or you as long as I'm here. I'll show him who's boss now." Kelly closed her eyes, trying to remember what it felt like to be hugged by her mum. Wondering if life had ever been soft and gentle and kind, or if it had always been like this. Someone wanting to hurt someone else, wanting to be top dog.

"It won't be long, Kel," Sean said, "till I can get us out of here. The guys I'm hanging with, they're like family. I look after them and they look after me – you'll be sorted."

"You know what that means," Kelly said. "They'll want you to do stuff. Drugs, knives, nicking and that."

"And what else do you think is going to get us out of this dump? We're better than this..." Sean looked around the room. "I'll get us out of here, Kelly, I swear. I'll take care of you, you know that, yeah?"

He'd held out his arms and Kelly had curled up next to him, not minding that she had to sleep on the bruised side of her face. That had been the last time anyone had hugged her. Two years ago, before Sean had almost killed that kid from Carter's gang and got put away. Two years since she'd seen those fleeting images of a woman in a negative, who might have been her mother.

The alarm on Kelly's phone beeped and she peeled her hand off the window, leaving behind another ghostly imprint of her palm. It was time to meet up with the others and go to Riverbank.

Bethan and Jay had come and found Kelly at lunch to tell her that Charlotte had called Jay last night and arranged to meet them at the back of Riverbank at ten o'clock this evening. Kelly'd been sitting with her old crew on a low wall by the wheely bins, where some of the girls went to smoke and try and catch a few rays on a rare sunny day.

Kelly knew that she'd arranged to meet Bethan for lunch, but when it came to it she had just fallen into step with the other girls, like she used to. It felt good, no need to think, no need to feel anything much.

"So you done with the geeks yet?" Yana had asked her, offering her some gum.

"Yeah, why you hanging with those losers, anyway?" Bea asked her.

"They're all right," Kelly shrugged, shaking her head when Yana offered her a ciggie.

"I don't mind Jay, to laugh at," Bea observed, "but that emo girl? She's just plain dumb."

"She's not," Kelly said mildly.

"So you're tight with her then, are you?" Yana challenged Kelly.

"No." Kelly reacted instinctively. "She's a laugh, though."

"You need to sort it, Kel, people are talking..." Yana said.

"What people?" Kelly interrupted.

Yana and Bea exchanged glances.

"We miss you, babe. You're not the same since—"

"Since what?" Kelly asked, intrigued to see if they would talk about Emily.

"Since that business with the dead kid," Yana muttered.

Bea nodded across the playground in the direction of Bethan and Jay. "Looks like Bella and Edward want you,"

Kelly sighed.

"Stay here and have a smoke."

"I don't smoke," Kelly said. "I'll sort this and then I'll be back, OK?"

"Sort what? What do you talk about?" Yana crowed.

"Nothing," Kelly called over her shoulder as she marched away.

When Kelly joined them, Jay was explaining that they couldn't arrive until the few teachers and pupils still at Riverbank would either be asleep or on the other side of the building, far away from the attic.

"And you're sure we have to go?" Kelly asked, crossing her arms and winking at Bethan. "If this is a curse, then what are we gonna do about it?"

"We have to try!" Jay's eyes flashed with unexpected anger. "She's just a kid like us, she doesn't deserve to die! This is someone's life we're talking about."

"All right!" Kelly said. "Bloody hell, calm down. You're a bit touchy, Jay."

Jay bit his lip hard as he stared at her. He seemed on the verge of saying something, but instead he shrugged.

"Whatever, it's nothing – I'm fine. I need to work out what to take up to the school tonight. We haven't got Hashim and his brother's car so big electrical equipment is out. Charlotte says that most of the school is walled in, but the grounds back on to the forest, so if we catch a bus to Hanger's Hill, there's this footpath that should take us up to the perimeter of the school. Charlotte says we'll know when we're near because there's a 'Trespassers Will Be Prosecuted' sign."

"I'm not sure about this," Bethan said, kicking at a stone

with the toe of her boot. "Hanger's Hill, by the bypass? That's really near where we found..."

"Emily," Kelly finished for her.

"OK, name me anywhere in this town where we aren't quite likely to bump into ghosts?" Jay countered.

"Plus, a bus out of town and then a hike through the woods in the dark?" Bethan said uneasily. "I went on the geography field trip when Bacon made us do orienteering. I don't like the countryside, it's not natural. I mean what if we get lost in the middle of the forest and the Woodsville Slasher gets us?"

Kelly snorted. "I'm with you on the whole forest thing – I don't really have the shoes for mud. But Beth, the Woodsville Slasher hasn't killed anyone in years!"

"That's not what the papers say." Bethan dragged that day's issue of the *Gazette* out of her bag and unfolded it with some difficulty against a rebellious breeze.

"SLASHER RETURNS TO PREY ON WOODSVILLE GIRLS" the headline screamed out from the page.

"There was a piece on it in my mum's *Daily Mail*," Bethan said. "And I heard a bloke in the lift saying Sky are sending down a news crew."

"But that's just mental," Kelly laughed, looking at Jay. "Tell her that's mental."

"It's possible," Jay said. "The Slasher killed kids, sixteen or under, which Charlotte is, and all her friends were. And he killed once a month. In four months: four girls dead. It's quite a coincidence, certainly enough to merit a police investigation."

"Yeah but—" Kelly interrupted Jay.

"*And* the slasher was never caught, just like Jack the Ripper. He just stopped killing. For years after the last Ripper murder, they never knew if he would strike again. The people of Whitechapel lived under his shadow, and he became like a demon, a ghost who could strike at any time."

"But the Slasher slashes with a knife!" Kelly insisted. "He's not called the Woodsville Crusher-stroke-Burner-stroke-Drowner, is he? If there's one thing I know from *Crimewatch*, it's that murderers don't change their MO. Besides, he'd be an old man by now. What's he going to do, stalk the streets on his zimmer frame?"

"We need to be scientific," Bethan added. "We know there are ghosts and quite a lot of them, but if we assume that everything we investigate..."

"Will you stop saying 'investigate', you are making us sound like losers!" Kelly complained, glancing over at Yana and Bea who were obviously talking about them.

"EVP," Jay said out of the blue.

72

"VPL?" Kelly countered, making Bethan giggle.

"Electronic Voice Phenomenon," Jay explained. Neither girl looked any the wiser. "Some people think you can record ghosts talking; sometimes in direct response to a question, sometimes replaying a dramatic event or sometimes just talking around you. In America they use it as a tool for paranormal research, there's loads of examples on YouTube. I'm pretty sure most of them are hoaxes, but there was this one a boy recorded by accident on a Civil War battlefield in Oklahoma. He was trying to record birdsong, but when he played back the tape there was a low male voice on it saying, *'Run and hide, Johnny.'*"

"Couldn't that just have been one of his mates, having a laugh?" Bethan asked.

"Well, he claims he was on his own and, get this, 'Johnny' was a slang name for Confederate soldiers, who were slain in their thousands on that field. The boy didn't know that until after he made the recording. Why don't we try to record EVP at Riverbank? We can't use a mobile because the signal will interfere with the recording, but Grandad's got a digital dictaphone. I bought it for him last Christmas when he was going on about writing his life story. I told him if he dictated on to it I'd type it up for him. It'd be perfect for recording EVP!"

For a fleeting moment Jay looked like his old self again, but then it was as if he remembered something terrible and his face crumpled in.

"Jay," Bethan said softly, putting her hand on his arm. "What is it? You've been so down. You can talk to us, you know, we're your friends, aren't we, Kelly, Kel?"

Kelly wasn't listening to her. Yana and Bea were whispering behind their hands, looking Bethan up and down as if she was dirt. If Beth didn't leave soon, they were going to have a go at her.

"Look, let's split. I'll see you at the bus stop about half nine, yeah?"

"No, meet us at Grandad's, an hour before that. We need to talk about some stuff," Jay called out, but Kelly acted like she hadn't heard him.

"EVP is a really good idea," Bethan said to Jay. "Where are you going? Want to hang out till bell?"

"No," Jay said flatly. "I've got to go. I need to find someone, see you later."

"Bye then," Beth called out as he walked away. Jay didn't reply.

It was freezing cold by the time Kelly finally made her escape to meet the others. She'd had to sneak out past her dad, snoring loudly in his chair, crushed empty cans at his feet.

For a moment, Kelly wondered what it would be like to live with just... parents. Normal people, who got on your nerves and in your face but didn't make it feel like your heart was going to explode out of your chest every time they came near you. Kelly pushed that thought to the back of her head. There was no point in thinking about something she would never have.

Kelly took her mobile out of her pocket and opened a new text, adding Hashim's name to it. The thing that she didn't want to tell anyone was that since Sean went down, the only other person who had ever made her feel safe was Hashim. Even with thousands of ghosts surrounding them, she'd not been afraid with him at her side. It stung her to admit how much she missed him.

She paused in the corridor, uncertain whether to text or not. Just as she was agonising over what to write, the hairs on the back of her neck crackled. But it wasn't the same feeling that she'd had in the café. Now she was instantly frightened.

It was quiet, too quiet. A few seconds ago the corridor had been filled with the muffled noises of people living: the thump of bass, the wail of a baby, the bark of a dog. Now there was nothing, not even the hum of electric lighting overhead, the kind of noise you only noticed when it stopped.

Even the sour smell that always lingered in the corridors combining with the scent of thirty different dinners had gone. As she stood there, stock-still, mobile phone in hand, Kelly felt like there was nothing but her and this corridor and if she opened any one of the doors that lined it, all she would find on the other side would be endless night.

There was someone, something behind her. With awful certainty, Kelly knew that it was edging down the corridor towards her.

You next, they said. But they didn't say when.

A light at the furthest end of the corridor went out and then another, and another. Kelly could feel the dark pressing at her back.

"Move," she told herself silently. "If you stay here..."

Her feet wouldn't budge, as the light directly behind her went out.

Kelly could feel their silent whispers, their fury and glee.

The light above her head snapped off.

"RUN!" She heard her own voice shout out as if at a great distance. It took what felt like every ounce of life she had left to rip the soles of her feet from the floor and push her rebellious body forward – it felt like it was coated in concrete. Frantically, Kelly pumped her legs, racing down the corridor, lights snapping out over her head, the dark and all it contained pursuing her. Instinctively she knew she didn't have time to wait for the lift, so she threw herself through the door to the stairwell, half expecting to tumble into nothingness. Instead she half-ran, half-fell down the first set of concrete steps, slamming in the brick wall at the bottom and propelling herself off of it with all her might to throw herself down the next flight. Still they were coming; dense, thick, black, swarming above her head. Again and again, Kelly stumbled down the steps, thumping into the wall, then throwing herself forward. For several long torturous minutes it seemed like she might be trapped on this stairwell forever: endlessly running, never safe. Finally she reached the ground floor and, praying that the fire door would open, she hurled herself against it, her burning lungs choking as they filled with the polluted night air, her body trembling with the effort it had been forced to exert. Noise exploded all around her; kids shouting, dogs fighting, boy racers pulling handbrake turns in the square, the hum of traffic beyond the estate. The smell of sour urine and a rotting bag of chips left by the doorway made her retch. But Kelly didn't care. All the noise and the stink and the bruises on her shoulders and scrapes on her skin meant that she was alive.

Gasping for breath, Kelly staggered away from the door and looked up at the tower she had just run down the best part of. Lights were on, glowing different colours behind a patchwork of curtains. It looked normal. It didn't look like the Army of the Dead had just been round; that they had been there, waiting for her. Waiting to... kill her. It dawned on Kelly that the ghosts were far more powerful than any of them had realised. And they wanted her dead.

She realised she was still clutching her phone, an empty text to Hashim waiting to be sent. Kelly knew better than anyone that there was no point in wanting someone who didn't want you, but that knowing that didn't make you stop wanting them.

"Meet us at Albert's? Miss u," Kelly typed in with her thumb. Then she deleted the last bit, and after another moment, she deleted the whole thing.

Maybe she did miss him and want him. But letting him know how she felt was another thing entirely.

CHAP✝ER FIVE

Bethan looked from Jay to Kelly as the lift they were standing in rattled its way up to Albert's flat. Kelly looked pinched, pale. Her full lips were colourless and her whole body seemed drawn in on itself. She'd barely said two words since they'd met. *Perhaps she's having doubts*, thought Bethan. Perhaps Kelly was trying to find a way to tell them she'd had enough of the geeky spook fest and that she wanted her old life back. But if that was what Kelly was thinking, then she'd say it. There was something else, something really dark dragging her down. Anxiously, Bethan wondered if Kelly's dad had done something again. It was scary, all the real-life everyday horror Kelly had to dodge at home. They hadn't talked about it, even though they knew he hurt her. Bethan didn't know how to begin. Casually, Bethan hooked her arm through

Kelly's and after a moment Kelly squeezed it briefly, never taking her eyes off of the floor.

Jay too was lost in his own thoughts, pain and sorrow etched on his face. *Why not me?* Bethan wondered. So far, although everything awful and shocking that had happened had invaded her life, her head and taken up every single spare moment that she'd had, still Bethan hadn't really been touched by it like the other three had. Weirdly, Bethan realised she felt jealous. Like even after everything that had happened, she was still an outsider.

Pushing that stupid thought away, she looked up at the floor numbers. The lift seemed to be extra creaky and slow today. She'd be perfectly entitled to have a lift phobia, she thought, after what happened with Carter and his mates. Bethan shuddered as she remembered the total terror that had engulfed her as she and Kelly had stood there, waiting for Carter to get in through the top of the lift and... Bethan didn't want to think about what would've happened if that lift engineer hadn't turned up when he did. But what, or who, had saved them that day?

The easy explanation was that the lift had already been playing up and someone had been stuck in it earlier but had got out long before the engineer turned up. But that didn't explain the footsteps that had chased them into the lift foyer, or the voice that told them to hide. They'd assumed it was Emily's mother – but knowing what they knew now, it could have been any ghost – and what's to say it was just one? Jay said that active spirits, who weren't tied to re-enacting the circumstances of their deaths over and over again, could move back and forward through time at will. Maybe a bad ghost had chased them into that foyer, knowing that Carter was going to be passing at that exact moment, herding them into a lift it knew wasn't working? But perhaps *another* ghost helped them out? What Bethan didn't understand was why none of the others seemed to want to answer any of the questions that had been left still hanging in the air.

Jay chewed the edge of his thumb, as the lift finally ground to a halt on Albert's floor and Kelly blinked when the bell pinged, as if she'd been daydreaming. Whatever they were caught up in, they obviously didn't feel like making her a part of it.

"Come on you two!" Bethan snapped as they sauntered out of the lift. "Look at the pair of you. You're walking around like zombies! We've got another case to solve and a load of other things we have to find out. We need to pull our socks up!"

Kelly and Jay stopped dead.

"Did you just say we need to pull our socks up?" Jay asked, the first hint of a smile playing round his lips that Bethan had seen in ages.

"Worse than that, did you just say we had a 'case to solve', Thelma?" Kelly snorted. "Bethan, we're kids off a council estate in a nowhere town. They aren't going to be making a movie of our lives. I bet that whatever is going to happen is just going to happen, and there won't be anything we can do about it."

"Is that what you really think?" Bethan challenged her. "Do you really mean we should just give up?"

"Well, it's not like we've exactly saved anybody's life so far, is it?" Kelly said.

"No," Jay said. "Although, I suppose you could say we saved someone's death."

"What's wrong with you two!" Bethan exclaimed. "We're supposed to be a team, you know, best buddies, working together. Why are you both being so useless?!"

Kelly looked at Bethan.

"Did you just call me useless?" Kelly's tone was mildly threatening.

"Yes, I flipping did," Bethan said, squaring up to Kelly. The two girls stared into each other's eyes for a long moment, and then in a heartbeat Kelly backed down.

"You're right, I've got other things going on. Things in my head. I wonder if it's even worth trying but... you are right. We have to try, what else can we do?"

Kelly thought about telling them about what had just happened in the stairwell, but somehow the words wouldn't come out of her mouth. Like really bad news you didn't want to break. The ghost army were here, and they could come at any place or time to grab them. "I suppose I haven't taken Charlotte and her dead friends very seriously. I'm sorry, Beth, I'm here now, OK? And I'm on it. I promise."

"And what about you, Jay?" Bethan said. "Half the time you seem like a ghost yourself!"

Jay's head snapped up and his eyes flashed, but he said nothing, only turning sharply on his heels to walk down the corridor to Albert's flat.

"A Ouija board?" Albert looked confused. "What were you doing, messing about with one of them things in Woodsville? What's this got to do with the ghost omen?"

"The what?" Bethan asked, but Jay interrupted.

"We didn't, Grandad, remember? It was that girl I just told you about, Charlotte Raimi. And now she needs some help sorting it out," Jay understated.

"You know about not letting strangers in, or talking to people you don't know on the internet, but you don't think twice about inviting a load of ghosts to mess with your head. You forget that people are just the same when they're dead as when they were alive, only more so. There are some nice ones, some boring ones and some angry, mad psychopathic ones. Funnily enough, it's not the ones who used to go to bed before ten with a mug of cocoa that queue up to get noticed at amateur séances. Now where's my dinner? Have you come to give me my dinner?"

Dismayed, Jay looked at a half-eaten cheese sandwich and cold mug of tea on the kitchen table. Normally Grandad's carer would have cooked him something at tea-time, but there didn't seem to be any washing-up.

"Grandad, didn't Eileen come round?"

"Her? She hates me, I told her to go away." Albert looked upset, and Jay glanced uneasily at the others.

"I'll put some beans on," Jay said.

"So, Mr Romero," said Bethan, getting Albert's attention. "Do you think the Ouija board could have cursed the Riverbank girls? That a demon or something could have cursed them through the Ouija board?"

"There is so much evil in the world, so much. But no, not a demon. Man made up demons to explain away evil, as if it isn't our fault. All the good and evil in the universe is in people, alive or dead."

"So you don't believe in God, then?" Bethan asked, surprised by how dismayed she felt.

"If there is a God, where is he?" Albert said bleakly, looking at Jay's back as he emptied the tin of beans into a pan. "The power behind creation can't be boxed up in one religion or the other and organised by a set of rules. It's people doing exactly that that has caused the most evil in this world since the beginning of time. Who is it that decides who is going to live and who is going to die? Why do the young die whilst an old useless body like mine goes on? Who knows the mind of God?"

"Right," Bethan said. She had been hoping to take notes, but so far nothing that Albert had said made any sense.

"OK, so say some bad-ass ghost came through the Ouija board – that would be enough to off some rich girls, yeah?" Kelly tried to steer the conversation back on track. "And if that's what's happened, then what do we do to send it back again? I'm guessing garlic and holy water's not going to do the trick."

"Garlic's for vampires, Kelly," Bethan grinned. "And it's not like they exist, anyway."

"Not round here anyway," Albert muttered.

"I know," Kelly rolled her eyes. "Not unless you count Victor Millers – the love-bite he gave Teri McKinn stayed on her neck for two weeks."

"Anyway," Bethan said, "so it would have to be a ghost?" Albert nodded. "And we have to somehow send it back through the board before it kills Charlotte, and the curse, if there is one, will go with it? Simple."

"If the ghost came through the board at all," Albert said thoughtfully. "A Ouija board is a dangerous thing, but it's not like a portal to another dimension. It's more like Twitter for ghosts."

"You've heard of Twitter?" Bethan said, amazed.

The weary, confused old man that Jay had been buttering toast for seemed to have gone and the old Albert was back again – but for how long, Jay worried, as he poured beans on to a plate and set them in front of his grandad. "I'm not dead yet, you know. I know about Twitter and that other thing… Myface. No, it's more likely that the Ouija board acted like a beacon, attracting the attention of a ghost already present. Riverbank Girls' School… that's an old building. Seventeenth century, if my memory serves me right. That's four hundred years of dead people right there. So really what you need to find out is which dead person it is."

"How will that help?" Bethan asked, her biro hovering over her notebook.

"Not sure yet," Albert admitted, his gaze settling first on the beans on toast and then on Jay. "What've you gone and done this for? I've had my tea!"

Bethan pursed her lips and put her pen down. Nothing was going right. Albert was all over the place and there was nothing solid or concrete that they could act on. She'd almost prefer to be doing some maths revision. At least you could look up the answers in books.

"Look," Jay said, anxious that people should stop asking his grandad stuff in case it upset him. "All we can do is get up there and see what's going on. Agreed?"

"Be careful," Albert said, forking up some beans and putting them in his mouth. "Curses are contagious, like a cold. Make sure you don't catch it."

"And how do we do that?" Bethan asked.

"Be careful what questions you ask." Albert focused on her with his one good eye, something Bethan always found very disconcerting.

"And there's another thing." Albert turned to Jay who was hunched over his grandad's dictaphone that he had found, still in its packaging, in the sideboard drawer. "You could ask it about the ghost omen, Jay," Albert said. "If it's a working Ouija board then you might be able to find him that way and talk to him. Find out if anything can be done."

"A ghost omen?" Bethan said.

"What the *hell* is that?" Kelly asked.

For what seemed like a long time, Jay was silent whilst he thought about how to tell Kelly and Bethan what, or rather who, he had seen. It may have been his ghost omen, his portent of almost certain death, but his other self had also warned him that others might die too, if Jay didn't act. And by others, surely he meant Bethan and Kelly.

Over the past few weeks, Jay had learnt what it was like to live with the threat of your own death hanging over your head. It was awful, like always waking up to take an exam you hadn't studied for, times by about a million. He couldn't get his head around the idea that today, or tomorrow, or next week sometime, something horrible and bloody and violent would happen to him and then he wouldn't be here any more; not like he was now, anyway. He'd be a ghost, at best something like Emily and at worst one of those hollow-eyed ghost soldiers. Kelly might pretend she was tough, but Jay wasn't sure she'd cope with losing someone else out of her life, and as for Bethan...

It was Bethan who called him three or four times an evening to ask him about a post on her blog or to research stuff for her; Bethan who sought him out at school and sat next to him in class, as if it was completely natural for a blue-haired girl to hang with a ginger geek who wore Tesco trainers.

He wasn't sure if he wanted her to 'like' him, though. It had always been Kelly for him – he couldn't imagine kissing any other girl, because he'd only ever imagined kissing her. And secondly, he didn't know how much longer he'd be around. It didn't seem fair to let someone like you when there was every chance you might die quite soon. Even though knowing that Bethan was pretending not to like him as much as she did made him feel happy, Jay couldn't do anything about it. Besides, she was at her best when she was focused, writing stuff down and looking stuff up.

So after exchanging a look with Albert, he told them almost everything. They didn't need to know that they could be in danger; and hopefully they would never have to know, if he found out what he needed to do to save them. As he talked, Jay knew for the first time in his too-short life what it felt like when your heart was breaking.

"No," Kelly was the first to break that silence after Jay stopped talking. "No, that's not right, you've got that wrong, Jay."

"It doesn't mean that you're going to definitely die, does it?" Bethan shook her head as she spoke, as if the movement might help her get the answer that she wanted to hear. Jay looked at Albert, who suddenly couldn't look at anyone, his face buried in his broken old fingers.

"Grandad's never heard of anyone surviving a ghost omen before," he said amazed by how calm he felt. "But I'm not giving up. What's the point of ghost omens even existing if they're not to warn you; if you couldn't change things? We're going to beat it, aren't we, Grandad?"

Albert forced a smile as he reached out and put his hand on Jay's knee. "Don't know what I'd do without you." His voice cracked and he turned his face away for a moment. "Don't know what I'll do."

"Jay." Kelly stood up and went and put her arms around her friend. "Listen, you are freaked out bad, you've seen your own ghost covered in blood. But what does that mean? Even if you didn't stick around to see if that omen had anything else to say, you know to be watchful, careful. Who says it was your blood? Who says it was even blood? Maybe you have an accident in a jam factory? Stay away from jam." Kelly smiled at Jay, trying to chase away his fear with bravado. She didn't realise that just the fact that Kelly King had put her arms around him gave Jay the strength to take on the world.

Jay looked Kelly in the eyes, and smiled. "Typical, it takes my certain death to get you to hug me." The pair of them laughed, warmth flowing between them.

Bethan stood up suddenly, and ran out of the room, her hand over her mouth.

"Watch him, watch him all the time," Albert told Kelly as she awkwardly removed her arms from Jay's shoulders and stuffed her hands into her pockets. "Fate's not something you can control; if it's meant to be, then it will be. It creeps up on you and takes you by surprise."

"Great," Kelly said. "Any other little cheery thing you'd like to share with us before we go and visit a four-hundred year-old house with a murdering ghost?"

"Get hold of the boy," Albert said. "The destroyer of evil. If there's anyone you need now, it's him. Hashim's important. Together you are very powerful."

"He's been blanking me for weeks, but I'll try calling him," Jay offered, then Kelly cut him off.

"No, I'll do it." She made a point of not looking at Bethan's tear-stained face as she came back into the room. "I'm just going outside to phone Hashim."

"Sorry, needed the loo," Bethan muttered, forcing herself

to look at Jay. "Nothing bad's going to happen, OK? I won't let it." Jay nodded. He could see that Bethan needed to believe that as much as he did.

Kelly stood in the corridor outside Albert's flat trying to forget about the last time she hung around in a corridor thinking about Hashim. She leant against the wall and looked for a second at a front door a few flats down from where she was standing. Soon after Hashim had first told them that he could see ghosts around him all the time, he'd told her that there was the ghost of a woman permanently outside that door, rattling at it, glancing over her shoulder as if something very bad was going to happen, desperate to get inside. She shuddered as the light above the haunted doorway flickered and the door trembled on its hinges. No wonder Hashim wanted to turn his face away from all the death that surrounded him. It was what she tried to do every day with her dad. It was just... well, why did he have to be such a bloody idiot about it?

She punched in Hashim's name and pressed call. It rang twice and then went to voicemail – he'd rejected her call. Kelly hesitated as the beep went. "Listen, there's this thing going down tonight at Riverbank Girls' School. We're going up there, getting a bus to Hanger's Hill and then sneaking in the back way through the woods at about ten. I know you don't want to know and I don't care one way or the other, but Jay and Bethan, they miss you. And Jay's in a lot of trouble. You might be the only person who can help him..."

Kelly hesitated. It felt there were a hundred words queuing up in her head that she wanted to say, like, "*I* miss you, *I* need you, it's not the same without you." But she refused to say them, tying her mouth into a tight angry knot until the threat of soppiness went away. "Like I said, I'm not bothered – but you know now anyhow." Kelly ended the call and looked again at the door still rattling on its hinges.

Whatever happened tonight, she got the feeling it wasn't going to be good.

CHAP+ER SIX

A fine, freezing drizzle had begun as soon as they stepped off the bus, filming their hair and faces like icy spider webs. Kelly wasn't thrilled, to say the least.

"OK, whose idea was this again?" she muttered miserably.

They had left the main road that ran up through the same forest that began or ended under the flyover only a little over half a mile away, and set off on the footpath that Charlotte had told them to follow. Already the forest had blotted out the lights from the road and it was near pitch black. The trees could just be made out, standing sentinel in the dark, like mute guardians, watching, waiting.

Kelly continued complaining, her voice echoing in the damp air, partly to cover the eerie silence, but also because here amongst the trees with a cloudy sky churning overhead, that feeling of hopeless terror threatened to come back and engulf her at any moment. Kelly knew that what had come for her earlier that night would come again, but she had no way of knowing when. Did the army of the dead wait for them to be alone? Looking or maybe even feeling vulnerable and weak? After all, when they came she had been thinking about her mother, nursing the sharp pain of her absence. When she was with Bethan and Jay she felt stronger; but maybe it was more than that. Maybe she *was* stronger. Maybe that's why they came after them one by one. *Me next*, she thought. Jay didn't have to worry because as long as she was OK, he would be too. There was no point in telling him or Beth what had happened to her. They each had their own private horrors to face. And Kelly knew only too well how to hide her bruises, the ones you could see and the ones she felt on the inside.

"I bet we could have walked in through the front door, no problem," she moaned. "I mean, the school's supposed to be half empty, isn't it?"

"This is the way Charlotte told us to come," Jay hissed back. He was holding his mobile out in front of him as a torch, but it only lasted a few seconds before it faded and died – and it hadn't lit up much anyway. He sighed. "Wish I'd thought of bringing a torch. I don't normally go to places that don't have street lights."

Jay crossed his arms against the cold. He didn't like the dark, not since he was a little boy and especially not now. Somewhere in amongst the trees, death could be lurking – and it could be his own.

"Am I the only one who thinks Charlotte is winding us up?" Kelly grumbled, as she felt water seep in through the toe of her fake Ugg boots, soaking her sock with freezing cold liquid. She wasn't dressed for a cold night, and her skin hurt. "I mean, Riverbank is more or less a prison for posh girls, right? Girls who cause trouble. We're taking her word on all of this. What's to say she even knew the girls that died? Maybe this whole thing is one big attention-seeking scam. She's virtually alone at a school where four girls have died, and her parents haven't even come to get her."

"That's harsh," Jay whispered. "But you're right. We should have Googled her. I don't know what's wrong with me, normally that's the first thing I'd have done."

There was a spell of silence, except for the squelch of mud, and the unnaturally loud sounds of breathing.

"Why is it so cold?" Bethan's voice echoed off the tree trunks. "It's supposed to be spring!"

"Summer never comes to Woodsville," Kelly only half joked, dragging her parka around her body and crossing her arms against the cold. It was almost true. The town was built in the middle of a deep dip, and although its slopes were gradual and barely noticeable, it was actually several hundred feet below sea level, resulting in Woodsville having its own mini-ecosystem: a fraction cooler, wetter and darker than the rest of the country. Spring arrived later here than anywhere else and when it did, it was a half-hearted affair that melted seamlessly into a wet, grey summer. Even at this time of year, nights were freezing in the woods. What little heat of day that had been absorbed into the forest floor now evaporated in the cold air, causing a thin mist to form at waist height, winding in and out of the trees like a living thing.

"If the ghost army hangs out anywhere, it will be here." Bethan shuddered. Her voice sounded oddly detached from her body in the disorientating dark, almost as if it had taken off on its own. She concentrated hard on where she was walking. They were following a footpath, but the trees grew so densely that it was criss-crossed with thick roots and studded with saplings. Beth couldn't stop picturing corpse hands bursting out from between the roots, grabbing at her ankles and pulling her into the mud.

"I read at the library that Woodsville Forest is the largest, most ancient forest left in Britain. Even though they cut a load of its trees down to build Woodsville town in the sixties, the trees keep coming back, sprouting up all year round in any little patch of earth they can find, even through concrete. Woodsville is the only council in Britain that has a department dedicated to cutting down saplings."

Kelly stopped dead and stared into the dark. "Something's out there."

Bethan and Jay stood perfectly still. As they waited, the rustle of the wind in the tree-tops that they hadn't noticed before, ceased.

Then there was nothing but the sound of their breathing.

"Do you think it's them?" Bethan whispered.

"I don't think it's anything," Jay said loudly. "Nothing at all!"

"Jay!" hissed Kelly.

"If it's my ghost," Jay said, "I don't want to put him off."

His fists were clenched at his sides, his knuckles glowing white, even in the dark. He couldn't stop thinking about what it would mean if he saw his ghost again. Jay felt like his life had all but stopped and he wasn't even dead yet. Maybe this was what dying was like, he thought. For a while everybody missed you, people cried and grieved. But then time went on, life went on. Perhaps because they knew that at some point quite soon, certainly before he got much older, he was going to die, they were getting used to the idea of him not being around in advance. Jay shook his head, trying to dislodge these dark thoughts. In the daylight, at school or at home with the TV blaring, he could forget about his ghost omen for a little while. But here in the forest, he wondered if every shadow was stalking him. If at any moment he'd come face to face with the image of his own death again. And if he did, how would he ever have the courage to stop and look it in the eye.

"Right, well…" Bethan went on, her voice quavering. "What if the trees were here for a reason? What if the reason that Woodsville is so haunted is because there's a hole here between this world and the next? Maybe the trees grow here to sort of mend the hole and when they get chopped down that's when things start to go wrong – what do you think, Jay?"

Bethan had stayed up late into the night, reading about Woodsville Forest and the environmental changes that occurred with the building of the new town. Slowly an idea formed in the back of her head and finally she'd managed to pin it down. She realised that the ghosts, the trees and the weirdness had to be tied into it. This area had always been more haunted than other places, but Jay's grandad said never as much as it had been in the last *forty years*. And forty years ago was when Woodsville new town was built. Bethan had planned on inviting Jay round for a coffee when her mum and dad were out, so that they might sit on the sofa and discuss this. But that was before Jay told about the ghost omen. The nights of daydreaming about certain boys and what might happen if she and one particular boy were to sit on her sofa were over. Now every second with Jay seemed important, even those in a freezing sodden forest; after all, perhaps something in her theory could help him too.

"Before the First World War," Bethan continued, hiding the wobble in her voice, as she jogged to catch up with Jay, "local people would never go into the woods, and I don't mean they wouldn't go in much. They *never* went into it – dating back as far as there are records."

"Yeah, I know that." Jay sounded unimpressed.

"At its largest, the forest covered over thirty square miles, but the local people never used it for hunting or foraging or grazing their livestock or anything. In a hard winter they'd rather go hungry than go into the forest to find food. The legend was that it was haunted with a legion of angry ghosts, and everyone believed it without question. An army of ghosts, Jay – sound familiar?"

"So you're telling me we're lost in a haunted wood," Kelly said, her scowl evident in the tone of her voice. "Of course we are. Brilliant. Why does nobody ever listen to me?"

"It's a theory," Jay said, a little edgily. "If a bit simplistic."

"Simplistic?" Bethan replied testily. "Just because you didn't think of it. Once, the forest had acted like a prison, it contained the overflow of dead – but now... they're out."

"If that was true, Grandad would have thought of it years ago. I mean, the Romeros are part of an ancient family of ghosthunters. I reckon we'd have figured out something so obvious by now."

"Yes, well sometimes you can't see the wood for the trees, like that fact that your grandad is barking mad," Bethan snapped before she could stop herself. "*You* can't see what's going on in front of your own face most of the time."

"And what's that supposed to mean?" Jay stopped and turned round so abruptly that Bethan bumped into him, her nose squishing against his chest.

"I mean... well, it's just... oh, what's the point!" Bethan tried to move past but he sidestepped to block her way.

"Go on, say it!" Jay challenged her.

"Look guys, we're in the middle of a creepy forest, yeah?" Kelly's voice cut through the air. "Now is probably not the time to be digging up the unresolved romantic tension, OK?"

"As if!" Bethan snarled, pushing her way past Jay.

"I don't know what you're on about," Jay hissed at Kelly before marching after Bethan. "But I do know that finding out about your imminent death is a bit of a buzz-kill, so excuse me if I haven't had the time to waste looking up the history of trees, because I'm a little bit busy trying to save our— my life!"

Kelly swore as she sank ankle deep into mud. "You owe me a new pair of shoes before you cop it, Jay-boy. And I swear if that Charlotte turns out to be a time-wasting psycho, I'm going to rip her head off—"

Kelly stopped in her tracks as they heard the crack of a breaking branch ring out as loud as gunfire somewhere amongst the trees ahead. It was followed in quick succession by a series of loud snaps and bangs that seemed to encircle them, shattering the eerie silence.

"What was *that*?" Bethan asked, in hushed tones.

"Foxes?" Jay sounded unconvinced as he peered into the thick gloom. "Although it would have to have been a very big fox."

"It won't be a fox," Kelly growled. "It's never a fox. Do you know, I'm just not in the mood for this tonight. I'm tired, my feet are wet, I have to listen to you two flirting... I'm not having this, simple as." She marched out into the middle of the footpath and yelled, "Who's there?"

A ricochet of noise surrounded them; creaking, snapping, thumping, rattling every branch. It sounded like the trees were shaking themselves awake and then, for a few seconds, it was as if the wood was filled with people talking all at once, a deafening wall of words. The breeze gathered into a wind, carrying on it moans and cries that built to a thunderous peak and then stopped, leaving an eerie and total silence. Like every sound had been sucked out of the night on an inward breath.

"Kelly!" Jay dragged the stunned girl back by her arm to huddle against the thick trunk of an elderly oak, pushing both girls behind him. One thing about knowing that you are going to die, was that it made you a whole lot braver.

"We should run, it's not far back down to the road on the footpath," Bethan whispered.

"Yeah, but which way?" In all the noise and confusion, Jay had lost his bearings.

A gust of wind rattled the branches above their head, just as a long thin howl came from somewhere in the trees. It didn't sound like a fox, or even a wolf. It was a human voice.

A human, howling.

"Let's just pick a direction and go in it," Kelly said. "Staying here isn't going to do us any good."

Bethan pushed her way past Kelly and Jay and pointed into the mist without speaking. A few metres away a light hovered about a metre off the ground, flittering in and out of the trees. It darted between the branches, disappearing for a few seconds and then reappearing metres away, and all the time the howling was growing louder and louder. The three pressed into each other, back to back as the trees seemed to mutter, and the shadows in their branches thickened and doubled and trebled, bristling with unfamiliar shapes.

The light blinked out again, reappearing much closer this time.

Bethan's voice trembled. "It's getting closer."

The three stood, huddled together in the opaque night, their wide eyes staring blindly, as every trace of light seemed to be extinguished except for the glow, which gradually grew nearer and nearer.

"Right," Jay said, "whatever happens, stick together. We can fight them off, we've done it before."

"Only by accident," Kelly snapped, her fear showing as

anger. "It's me they said they want next, and I don't get any fancy omen to tell me about it. And anyway, you didn't fight them off, Hashim did, and he's not here!"

"Yes he is." Hashim stepped out from the shadows. The three stared as he waved a powerful torch in front of him, like a little boy playing Star Wars. It took them several seconds for the fear and adrenalin to begin to ebb away. "Had you lot freaked out, didn't I? I scared you all to death! Useless load of ghosthunters you are, scared to death by a flipping torch!"

"You came!" Kelly felt a rush of happiness as she took a few steps towards him, and then halted as an altogether different emotion hit her. "You bloody moron! I swear I'm going to...!"

"Kiss me?" Hashim said. "Seriously Kel, can you stop calling me all the time? I know you like me, but get the hint, yeah? It's not going to happen."

Kelly was stunned into silence, the rage and hurt bubbling up in her chest eclipsing all of the fear that she'd felt only a few seconds earlier. She'd been so pleased to see him, and then he made her look like a fool. She shook her head, biting back the torrent of words she knew he was trying to get out of her.

"You know what," she said, "you're not worth it."

"Mate, I'm glad you came," Jay greeted Hashim, so relieved that he didn't have to fight off an army of ghosts or face his own death that his initial anger evaporated completely. "You really had us scared there, good one!" Jay nodded at Hashim's backpack. "Don't suppose you've got your laptop and some monitors in there, have you?"

"No, I've got some Pringles and some Diet Coke, though. And a spooky torch... *whooooooooo!*" Hashim held the torch under his chin so it cast weird shadows on his face, making him look like someone else entirely.

"Can we just shut up and get on with this?" Kelly growled. "Which direction?"

"That way." Hashim pointed up the footpath and the group walked on, Kelly stalking ahead, closely followed by Jay.

Bethan linked her arm through Hashim's and gave it a squeeze. "It's really good to have you back," she said. "Even if I could kill you for scaring my socks off."

"I'm not back," Hashim told her, shrugging her arm off. "Kelly left a message, said Jay was in some kind of trouble..." He raised his voice so that Kelly would be able to hear him. "And I'd never miss an opportunity to break into a girls' school, I bet those babes haven't seen a bloke in months."

"Hashim!" Bethan lowered her voice as she watched Kelly marching ahead. "Look, I get that you're freaked out; we all are. But what's Kelly ever done to you?"

"I'd only be hurting her if she was bothered, and she's not," Hashim shrugged. "And anyway, I'm not freaked out. I'm fine, it's all good."

"Are you joking me?" Bethan tried to make out Hashim's expression in the dark. "It must be worse for you than anyone. You see them, all the time, all around you. It's a wonder you haven't gone mad."

"You know what?" Hashim told her. "If you practise, it gets like so you almost don't notice them, like they're just another face in the crowd. That's what I do now. I've almost forgotten they're there and that's the way I like it."

"Then why are you here?" Bethan asked him.

"I told you, a girls' school..."

"Why are you *really* here?" Bethan pressed him as the group drew to a halt, stopping at a chipped and mouldy 'TRESPASSERS WILL BE PROSECUTED' sign.

"Is Jay really in trouble?" Hashim whispered, so that the others couldn't hear him. Bethan nodded, dropping her chin. Hashim shrugged. "That's why."

"Right." Jay peered round the sign. "Charlotte said there was a hole in the wire fence behind the... yes, it's here. We head across the field and she's going to meet us in the chapel."

"Oh good, let's hope there's a graveyard too," Kelly snarled as she made her way through the fence, followed by Jay. "That would really make my day."

"The light was a good trick, but a bit obvious," Bethan told Hashim as he held the wire fence apart for her to climb through. "I wouldn't have ever fallen for it if you hadn't scared us with all that other stuff."

"What other stuff?"

"The trees rattling, the voices in the dark and the howling and the moans from everywhere? How did you do that?" Bethan asked. "Did you, like, rig up some ropes and pulleys and bring a sound-system or something?"

"Voices? Rattling? What are you talking about, babe?" Hashim said. "I only had the idea of messing around with the torch at the last minute."

"Yeah, yeah..." Bethan turned to grin at him as he followed her through the fence but the expression on Hashim's face was deadly serious.

"I'm telling you, Beth, whatever that was – it wasn't me."

Riverbank chapel was set a little way apart from the main school. It was a small, squat building, a hunched shadow against the rapidly clearing night sky, a half moon casting a silvery light on it. Much to Kelly's delight, there were no gravestones and they could see a flickering glow through the chapel door, that had been left slightly ajar.

"Hello?" Jay called quietly as he pushed the heavy wooden door open with a long loud creak. For a moment it looked like the chapel was empty, but then he saw Charlotte with her back turned, bent over something he couldn't see. "Charlotte?"

She jumped, as if she'd been caught in the act, and greeted them with a smile.

"Hello, you!" she called cheerfully, clearly not at all fazed by sneaking out of school and breaking into the chapel in the middle of the night. It was bravado that Jay couldn't help but be drawn to. They had a lot in common, him and Charlotte Raimi, he thought. Both young, and facing death. Despite what Kelly said, Jay liked her. Knowing you might be about to die horribly at any minute was enough to make anyone act a bit strangely.

"How were the woods, good and scary?" Charlotte beamed as she walked up the aisle to meet them.

"Funny you should mention that..." Jay grinned, but before he could go on Hashim stepped in front of him and picking up Charlotte's hand, kissed the back of it. Wincing,

Bethan looked at Kelly, whose glare was as hard as stone, but it bounced off Hashim's back unnoticed.

"Pleased to meet you, I'm Hashim." His smile was quite charming and Charlotte returned it with a flutter of lashes. "You'll be fine now I'm here," Hashim reassured her.

"I'm glad you're here," Charlotte replied softly. "I've heard all about you."

"Have you?" Jay asked, wondering when and how. Was Hashim really the legend amongst the girls of Woodsville he was always claiming?

"So why are we meeting here then?" Kelly barged into the conversation. "This isn't where you held the séance, is it?"

"No." Charlotte's smile faded as she noticed Kelly. "I thought this would be a good place to wait for you, where we could meet without being noticed." Charlotte pushed her hands into her pockets and looked up at the vaulted ceiling. "We have to come here every morning for assembly, even though this building hasn't been consecrated for nearly a hundred years."

"Consecrated?" Bethan asked, looking at Jay.

"When a church or a temple is built it's usually blessed and made holy, God's house," Jay explained absently as he watched Charlotte. She was looking around the chapel like she had never sat in it before.

"You like ghost stories, huh?" Charlotte said. "Well, I've got one for you. This place was ordered to be built by Rupert Godfrey, lord of the manor and the local magistrate back in... 1649. The year good King Charles got beheaded and the country went Puritan."

"Don't tell me, King Charles marches around here with his head tucked under his arm," Kelly barked. "Can we get on with it? And for the record, I'm going home through the front gate. I don't care who sees me."

Charlotte eyed Kelly. "Typical chav – never interested in learning anything. Godfrey was appointed local magistrate at the same time as the chapel was commissioned. During his first year he hung twenty-four local people in the woods you walked through. Eighteen of them for witchcraft."

"Witchcraft!" Kelly snorted. "Cobblers."

"You think so, do you?" Charlotte's laugh sounded out of place in the chapel. "No one thought that back then, everyone thought it was real, and it was like an epidemic..."

"Our old friend, mass hysteria again," Jay said, enjoying Charlotte's weird little sideshow despite himself.

"Witches had to be stamped out and it was Godfrey who stamped them out round here. And everyone he hanged was buried where their rotting corpses fell, in the forest,"

Charlotte went on. "Because if you were executed, you didn't get buried in consecrated ground."

"In the woods you just made us walk through?" Jay asked, starting to feel uneasy.

"But I thought nobody went into the woods," Bethan queried her. "I didn't think anyone went in the woods back then?"

"They shouldn't have." Charlotte turned to Bethan, her blue eyes glittering in the candle light. "But they did on Godfrey's orders. The story goes that every single man that dug graves in the woods was dead within the year. Godfrey never lived to see this chapel finished, even if there is an effigy of him back there." Charlotte nodded to where a stone tomb topped with a reclining sculpture of a man, his hands seemingly folded in his lap, could be made out in the flickering light. "Some say on a quiet night you can see him wandering in and out of the trees, looking for a way home. But he'll never get there, the witches won't let him. Did you get scared in the forest, Kelly?"

Kelly scowled.

"Well you're all ghosthunters, aren't you? I thought you'd enjoy it. See anything good?" Charlotte grinned.

"I knew it. I knew this whole thing was a wind-up. Don't you know we've got far more important things to do than entertain a stupid stuck-up little bitch like you? Do you realise how dangerous it is out there? I'm going."

"No, please! Don't." Kelly turned back to Charlotte and suddenly she looked like a different person, the easy smile had vanished and she looked terrified at the thought of them leaving.

"Look, I'm sorry. I don't know what's wrong with me. I just, I'm so scared that... it's like nothing matters any more. It doesn't matter if I get caught, it doesn't matter if you lot hate me. Nothing matters because..." Charlotte trailed off.

"It's OK, we get it," Jay reassured her.

"I don't," Kelly muttered. She'd tried not to hate Charlotte, but it was impossible. Everything about her was off. "I don't get why sometimes you seem to be scared out of your skin and others... well, it's like you're enjoying this."

Charlotte stared at her, speechless.

"Did we really need to come through the woods?" Jay asked Charlotte. "I mean, if the school's half empty, what's the difference?"

"I don't know... I... I wanted you to take me seriously, to see that I'm not making this stuff up! I thought if you got spooked before you got here, it might help."

"Don't you get it?" Kelly marched over and stuck her face in Charlotte's. "There's more than enough real scary stuff going in this town to last us a lifetime, which might not be very long. This might be a game to you, but it isn't to us!"

"Please," Charlotte cowered.

"Kelly, back off." Hashim pushed his way between them. "Leave the lady be."

He slipped his arm round Charlotte who still stared at Kelly, her blue eyes wide.

"Lets just get this over with, shall we?" Jay said. "What's the best way into the attic?"

Kelly didn't listen as Charlotte began to explain to Hashim, Bethan and Jay. Still stung by Hashim's intervention, she wandered to the back of the chapel, to the tomb of that dead Godfrey bloke that Charlotte had been hunched over when they had found her. Kelly got an odd feeling as she approached the tomb, as if it wasn't a cold piece of stone but the actual dead body of the man it had been sculpted to represent. For a second it was almost like she could see his corpse laying there, long hair flowing over a lace collar, stiff hands folded neatly on his chest. Kelly held her breath as she took a final step closer and looked down on the face of the dead man and gasped.

Someone had taken a marker pen to the centuries old statue, blackened out the eyes so they looked like empty sockets in a skull and drawn a single tear on its alabaster cheek. Most shockingly of all, a jagged wound was slashed across its neck, black blood seeping out. Turning round slowly, Kelly watched Charlotte looking like a lost little girl.

Something about her was really, really wrong.

CHAPTER SEVEN

"This is where we did it." Charlotte gestured to an open expanse of floorboards in the middle of a cluttered attic. Charlotte flicked on a light switch, igniting two naked bulbs that spluttered and stuttered for a few moments before emitting a steady thin glow of pale yellow light. It cast long, twisted shadows thrown by the maimed and dismembered furniture across the floor and ceiling.

The four stood looking down at the space that Charlotte and her friends must have cleared, directly under one of the lights. The rest of the attic was covered in thick dust, ancient cobwebs tangled in every nook, but here there were streaks of clean floorboards showing through the grime, where old furniture or boxes had been pushed and pulled aside, and even, Kelly noticed, a small handprint where Charlotte or one of her friends had been kneeling on the floor. In fact, it was so tiny, it couldn't have been Charlotte's – she had hands like a builder. Kneeling down to take a closer look, Kelly noticed chalk markings on the floor. Someone had tried to rub them out, but they were still there.

"Hey, what's this?" she asked, pointing at the chalk.

"We drew a pentagram on the floor," replied Charlotte. "Tara said a five-pointed star would help protect us from anything bad coming through, just in case... but it didn't seem to work."

"No wonder," Bethan said, crouching down next to Kelly and tracing a finger along the scuffed chalk line. "An open pentagram is like a call to arms, a challenge. You need a closed pentagram for protection, one with a circle drawn around the five points. You did the exact opposite to shielding yourselves from harm – you invited it in."

"And how do you know that, weirdo?" Kelly asked her mildly, raising an eyebrow.

Bethan looked embarrassed. "Well last year, I sort of thought about joining this Wiccan thing, but it was a bit lame, so I gave it a miss and took up learning to play bass instead. Then it turned out I'm not so musical, so I was about to start writing a novel when.... well, when I started hanging out with you lot and none of that stuff seemed very important any more."

"Isn't Wiccan like uber-Goth witch?" Kelly asked her, mortified. "You wanted to be a *witch*? You must *never ever* let anyone know about this. The kids at school will rip you to shreds."

"I don't know, I think it's pretty cool," Charlotte said, smiling at Beth, suddenly warm.

"It was only for about five minutes," Bethan explained. "There were a lot of coven meetings, I thought it might interfere with my coursework."

"Oh my God, there is no helping you," Kelly scoffed. "You might as well become president of the chess club while you're at it and then I'll tell everyone you're my best friend and we can commit social suicide together."

"I'm your best friend?" Bethan beamed at Kelly, then something caught her eye. "Hang on, there's something else down here..." She reached under an upturned chair and picked up something small, that caught the light. "A crystal?"

Bethan held out the small, jagged piece of pink quartz in the palm of her hand for the others to see.

"Yes, Tara brought them – she said they'd act like another shield between this world and the next," Charlotte explained.

Bethan shook her head.

"That's not what crystals do, they're like amplifiers. Some Wiccans believe they make spells stronger, make magic more powerful. Even give spirits the added energy they need to manifest."

"Wow, this Tara chick got it really wrong," Hashim said, winking at Charlotte, but this time she didn't respond.

"Tara looked it up on Wikipedia, she said she knew everything we had to do to make the séance look real and keep us safe..." Charlotte trailed off.

"Hang on a minute," Kelly cut across her. "You're a liar, and you know what, I'm sick of it. I'm sick of you being all 'oh no, save me' one minute and then acting like it's all posh girl larks the next." Kelly walked across the smudged pentagram, and towering over the smaller girl, stuck a finger in her face. But instead of cowering, Charlotte squared up her shoulders and stuck out her chin, refusing to back down. For a moment she looked like she'd actually enjoy a fight.

"When we met you in town you made it seem as if you found the Ouija board and had a go on it there and then, without thinking about it or planning it," Kelly challenged her. "But if Tara went off and looked up pentagrams and crystals, then that's not true. What's the real reason you've got us here, Charlotte? Because I tell you what, I've got enough problems without chasing round after some psycho rich kids."

Scared, lost Charlotte faded for a second and even Jay saw the flash of anger that ignited in her eyes as she glared at Kelly. But it disappeared as quickly as it came, leaving Charlotte blushing and shamefaced.

"Yes," she admitted. "Yes, I did lie. I promise you it happened the way I said it did, honestly – only when we tried the board out on the night we found it, nothing happened. We just messed around for a while and... it was boring. Everything is so boring here, nothing ever happens. I mean it's a four-hundred-year-old house and there's not even any good ghosts..." Charlotte looked perplexed as Jay, Bethan and Kelly turned to look at Hashim.

"She's right," he confirmed. "I've seen nothing tonight."

"I see ghosts," Hashim explained, a bit embarrassed. "Everywhere I go, mostly. But not up here, not at the moment, anyway..."

"That's so interesting," Charlotte smiled at him. "It must be a terrible burden."

"Like water off a duck's back," Hashim boasted.

"So?" Kelly cut in, wondering why no one else was as irritated by Charlotte's constant play-acting as she was. "What really happened?"

"We talked about it for a couple of days, about how we could pull a prank on some of the other girls. Make them believe that the Ouija board really worked. Tara found out about the crystals, and the pentagram. She even went out and got some special plants from somewhere: lavender, nightshade, lovage and this weird little rooty thing... looked like a little person."

"Not mandrake?" Bethan asked her.

"That's it," Charlotte nodded.

"But mandrake doesn't even grow in this country, it's far too cold here, unless..."

"Unless?" Jay asked.

"Well, Wiccans believe it grows in the blood of someone who's been... hanged," explained Beth.

"Tara said she found all the plants growing right here in the woods," Charlotte said. "I remember thinking she was just winding us up because lavender is a summer flower."

"Well, we don't know that she had real mandrake – it could have been a bent parsnip or something," Bethan said thoughtfully. "Even so, it sounds like Tara knew a lot more about this stuff than just looking it up on the internet. Those plants are all supposed to thin the barriers between the living and the dead, which might have no effect anywhere else, but in Weirdsville..."

"It's party time for the departed," Kelly finished. "Do you think Tara knew that?"

"No," Charlotte shook her head. "Tara's like a sister to me – we shared a room, we shared everything. She is... was my best friend. I'd have known if she was messing around with anything like that. She liked to have fun and she thought pranking the other girls would be hysterical, but she wouldn't lie to me." As Charlotte finished speaking the light above them dipped and flickered. Jay and Hashim exchanged a glance. It could just be dodgy electrics, but after Emily they knew that a ghost attempting manifestation would draw on any power source it could, electrical or even human.

"Keep looking," Jay told Hashim. He slipped the digital recorder he had borrowed from Albert's out of his pocket and, setting it on top of a pile of boxes, pressed record. "Maybe this will pick up some EVP." Charlotte looked at him. "Ghosts talking. Recording devices like this can pick up on what human ears can't, because they work on a frequency that humans can't hear. Go on, keep explaining."

"The night it happened, we came up here to practise our prank," Charlotte began. "We had a plan to stick some clear wire on to the pointer and to make it look as if it was moving around on its own. When we'd had a few goes, got it down, we were going to get some of the other girls up here and scare them to death . . . it was going to be so funny. That was when everything happened, just like I told you it did in the café, I promise."

"Why didn't you tell us all this in the first place?" Jay asked her. "Why lie?"

"Look, I haven't been able to get anyone to take me seriously. The school don't want to know, and do you think Ofsted are really going to think that four girls have died because of a ghostly curse? If I talk to any adults they'll think… they'll think I've gone crazy and lock me up. I wouldn't believe me – would you?" There was dead silence in the room. "I thought if I told you that we had been planning a prank that you would tell me where to go. But my friends *are* dead. And I really believe that I'm next." Charlotte's voice wavered and tears welled in her eyes.

Slowly Kelly began to clap. "Are you head of the school drama club by any chance, because that performance could win you an Oscar. I'm done with this crap. I'm going home. Who's coming? Beth?"

"Wait…" Hashim interrupted her, his face suddenly tense. Everybody stood perfectly still.

"What?" Jay asked him. "Can you see something?"

"No… it's weird, it's like I can feel it. There's something here, not a ghost exactly but… something like one."

"Are you winding us up again?" Kelly demanded, irritably.

"No, no – I've never felt anything like this before." Hashim looked very slowly around the room, searching every nook and crevice with his gaze. "I feel as if something is here, waiting. Like, on the other side of a door. It wants to come through but it can't open it by itself, it's waiting for us to."

There was a beat of silence as each of the others digested what Hashim had told them.

"Well, let's stick a bolt and a chain on the door and go home," Kelly said, starting for the stairs that led down from the attic.

"Wait," Jay stopped her. "Kelly, don't go, we need you. I need you."

Kelly stopped in her tracks, then slowly turned and looked at Jay.

"Look," Jay explained. "If there's something 'ghostly' waiting, then it might mean Charlotte wasn't completely lying. If we try using the Ouija board again, then maybe we can find out what happened to the other girls and stop it from happening to Charlotte."

"Personally, I don't care what happens to Charlotte," Kelly told him.

"And *maybe*," Jay went on. "Maybe I can use it to find..."

He glanced at Charlotte. "Well, what I need to find. And if I'm going to do that, then I need all my friends around me, especially you, Kelly. I can't do it alone."

"Especially me?" Kelly hesitated. "Are you hitting on me?"

"No, no! You're stronger than me, that's all."

Kelly sighed, and dropped her bag on the floor with a heavy clunk.

"Does this mean you are going to help me?" Charlotte begged, and when Kelly looked into her eyes she knew she was looking at genuine fear. The more she hung around Charlotte, the less she understood her. Kelly would be glad, really glad, when she never had to set eyes on her again.

"So what should we do?" she asked Jay.

He turned to Charlotte. "We need the board."

They all knelt on the floor and watched as Charlotte re-drew over the faded pentagram.

"Don't forget the circle to contain it," Bethan reminded her and Charlotte drew around the five points of the star, skimming it so lightly as it passed Kelly's knees that Bethan picked up the chalk and went over it again. The three girls sat back as Hashim and Jay carried over the board and set it in the middle of the star.

"So what happens next?" Jay asked Charlotte. "You need to do everything the same way that you did that night."

Charlotte twisted round on her knees and pulled a plastic carrier bag out from where it had been stuffed behind a huge old trunk with R. M. embossed on it in gold. "We didn't use all the plants that night..." She pulled a dried and crumbly sprig of lavender out of the bag and looked at Bethan. "Should I put these down?"

"Um, I don't think we need to make the veil between us and them any thinner than it already is," Bethan said, glancing at Jay, who nodded in agreement.

"OK, well each of us sat at one point of the star," Charlotte told the others. "Jay, Hashim?" She invited the boys to sit either side of her, which Kelly thought was just about typical.

"Do we get to hold hands?" Hashim grinned at Charlotte, who smiled back, her eyes glittering with excitement.

"Afraid not," she told him. "We each put a finger on the planchette. Just very lightly, so that you don't move it by mistake." They all leant forward over the board, bringing their faces very close together.

"Then what?" Jay asked in a soft voice.

Charlotte paused and then lifted her chin a little. "Spirits of the Dead, if you are present come forth and declare yourselves." As she finished speaking she sucked in her breath and held it.

All five of them waited.

"Just a thought," Kelly said after a few seconds. "We'd better hope that this doesn't work. The last thing we need is a curse of doom, following us round, hey Jay?"

"We haven't got the plants out and we've enclosed the pentagram, so whatever does come through, it shouldn't be as strong this time," Bethan told Kelly.

"Nothing is what will happen if you two don't stop chatting," Jay told them.

As he spoke, all of them looked up, glancing at each other to show that they sensed the same thing. A palpable tension, as if the air in the room had thickened.

Then the planchette moved across the board and stopped on the word: *Yes*.

"Who moved that?" Kelly said, looking at Charlotte. "Was it you?"

"Hashim?" Jay asked. "Anything?"

"I don't know." Hashim looked unsettled. "I feel like something is pressing, pressing into the air around me. You can feel it too, right? Unhappiness... no, more than that... unfairness. I can't see anything, but I can feel it, really strong. And if you can feel it too, that means that either the board must be working already or this spirit... emotion, is very powerful."

"Charlotte, Kelly and Hashim, take your fingers off the planchette," Jay instructed, impressed that all three obeyed him. Now just Jay and Bethan had their fingers on it, tips touching, their faces very close together.

"Is there anybody there?" Jay said, looking into Bethan's eyes as he spoke.

They looked down as the planchette moved to the centre of the board and then back again to *Yes*.

The atmosphere in the room transformed instantly. Cold leached out of the corners and chilled the air, and although Bethan was too afraid to take her eyes off Jay, she got the impression that the shadows cast by the weak light-bulb had doubled in her peripheral vision.

"Wow." Hashim stared around him. "We are not alone, any more. There are a lot of people here... maybe thirty, at least."

"The ghost army?" Kelly asked, her voice strangled with fear.

"No, they look different, like people still. Some are smiling, some aren't. But they're normal, you know, for dead people."

"What do we do?" Bethan asked, staring at Jay.

He looked blank at first, but then he had a thought. "Is there anyone there who looks... familiar?"

Hashim hesitated, looking sideways around the room, thinking, *what are you on about, mate? It's a crowd of ghosts, not a family photo.*

"No, not Emily, if that's what you mean. There is a girl here, though, standing behind Charlotte. She looks very frightened, long brown hair. She's holding a broken necklace in one hand."

"Tara," Charlotte breathed, her eyes wide. "Tara, come forward!"

Anger crackled in the cool air, not rage exactly but a kind of frustration and helplessness. For a second, all of the living people there understood exactly how terrible it was to be trapped in death, not moving forward or crossing over to the next dimension, unable to escape or even complain.

"Can't you talk to them?" Charlotte asked Hashim urgently.

"No, even if this lot wanted to, they couldn't. They're being held back by something. It's like they're not quite active spirits or imprints, not in this dimension or the next. They're... prisoners."

"Tara, are you OK?" Charlotte asked the board, as if she

were afraid that if she looked she'd see her friend standing over her.

The planchette slid quickly from letter to letter, so fast that Bethan's finger slipped off it, and Jay withdrew his with a sharp intake of breath. "It stung me," he said. "Like static electricity."

All five stared at the planchette as it moved, completely alone, scampering across the board at speed from one letter to the next: *T. R. A. P. P. E. D.*

"By who? How? Tara, what happened?"

Kelly watched Hashim's eyes, following something else. "It's too much, I'm losing control, there are too many," he muttered.

The planchette slid quickly from word to word, almost skidding off the board in its urgency to get its message across, now grazing across a jumble of letters that didn't make any sense.

"This is bad," Hashim said. "They're angry, fighting for a turn to come through." He stared at the out-of-control planchette. "This is going to get worse."

A chair screeched across the floor knocking so hard into Bethan that she fell forward into the pentagram.

"Ow!" She sprang up. "It burns!"

A book sailed through the air past Kelly, narrowly missing

her head, and the trunk lid behind her slammed over and over again.

"Do something!" Kelly yelled at Hashim, who seemed mesmerised by the chaotic planchette.

"You!" he said pointing at the air above Charlotte's head. "You may speak."

The planchette halted and the trunk stopped slamming. For a moment, nothing happened. And then the planchette moved again, more slowly this time.

Y. O. U .N. E. X. T.

As soon as it touched the final *T* it flipped into the air and landed in Kelly's lap. She flung it back on to the board.

"She's pointing," Hashim said, turning away, shielding his face as if he couldn't bear what he was looking at.

"At who?" Kelly demanded. "Who's she pointing at?"

But before Hashim could answer the planchette began to move again.

S. H .E .I. S. C. O. M. I. N. G. F. O. R. Y. O. U.

"Who is she, and who is she coming for?" Charlotte asked with bated breath, but the planchette remained still. No one moved a muscle.

"Oh no," Hashim said, tears glistening in his dark eyes.

A wave of utter sadness swept the room, filling every corner with regret and despair, like every loss, pain and hurt that anyone had ever felt had been distilled into that moment. It felt like each one of them had had their hearts wrenched out of their chests.

Kelly pressed her hands over her ears as if she could blot out something she couldn't hear but could only feel, vibrating deep in her chest.

"They're crying," Hashim said. "Tara, the others – the spirits, they're all crying. I can't bear this." He stood up, tears streaming down his face. "You have to go. We can't help you. You can't stay here, go back. Go back into the shadows, I command you, go back!"

In that instant the digital recorder flew off the boxes and landed with a thud several feet away. As soon as it hit the ground, all the sadness that had been suffocating them dissolved into thin air. Bethan flung herself into Kelly's arms and the two girls held each other. For a second, all five waited, tense, for that moment that always comes just when you relax, the moment when you get caught off guard. Then gradually, Bethan and Kelly let go of each other and Jay climbed to his feet, rubbing his palms over his face. Finally, Hashim walked over to the recorder and picked it up.

"They weren't like any ghosts I've ever seen. It was awful."

Bethan nodded at the digital recorder. "Should we listen to it?"

Hashim handed it to Jay, anxious to be rid of it.

"Well, I need to go home and download it on to my computer, take off our voices and clean up the background noise, before we know if we've got anything, but..." Jay fiddled about with the recorder for a moment. "This is the last minute before it fell off the boxes."

He pressed play and they heard their own voices, then Hashim's loud and clear as a bell. Then they heard something on the tape that they hadn't heard in the room. A girl's voice thick with tears and fear, sobbing.

Charlotte clapped her hand over her mouth in horror. "That's Tara," she whispered through her fingers.

Abruptly, Hashim walked to the top of the steps. "I'm off," he said. "I don't know why I came here tonight. I don't need any of this."

"But mate, we need you," Jay said. "We can't do this without you."

Hashim turned round, his face drawn and pale.

"If I stay, I have to face the things I see, and I don't want to. Maybe this time next year we'll all be dead, but if that's what's going to happen then, I'm pretty sure we can't stop it. So I want to have a laugh, kiss some girls, and play footy, before it's too late. What I *don't* want is to be followed around by freaks!"

And Hashim pointed at the space above Charlotte's head.

"You're seeing a ghost right now, aren't you?" Kelly gasped. Hashim seemed to struggle, as if he was uncertain of what he should say.

"It's my ghost – the one who follows me – the man in the long black coat." He looked down at Charlotte. "You need to be very afraid. Make sure you're never alone, don't go places where accidents can easily happen."

"What?" Charlotte asked him, terrified. "What have you seen?"

"Trust me," Hashim said as he thumped down the stairs. "You don't want to know."

CHAPTER EIGHT

*I*t had been a long time since they'd met up in the old history block, Bethan realised, as she waited for the others to arrive after the school bell sounded.

After their experience at Riverbank, true to her word, Kelly had left a pale and shaky Charlotte and marched out of the front gates of the school. Unsure of where Hashim had got to, Bethan and Jay had followed Kelly in silence, neither one of them fancying chancing the woods again. The sun was almost up, smouldering somewhere behind a steel-grey sky, when they finally trudged into the outskirts of Woodsville. Bethan had been glad, for once, to see the cool calm vistas of cracked concrete, the sedate towers of her estate watching over them as they trailed wearily towards its grubby embrace.

"Going to school?" Bethan asked the other two as they halted at the crossroads that would split them up. According to Bethan's watch, registration was due in just over three hours.

"Might as well," Kelly said. "I sleep better in class than I do at home."

"I'm not going to get any sleep anywhere," Jay said, looking around him with red-rimmed eyes.

"Hey, chin up, ginger," Kelly said, winding her arm around Jay's neck with the kind of ease that Bethan envied and planting a fat kiss on his cheek. "So when are we going to meet?"

"Straight after school, history block?" Jay suggested.

"Really? Because we haven't been there since..." Bethan got the feeling that no one was listening to her.

"Fine," Kelly said. "Later."

"Bye," Jay said to Bethan a little awkwardly, and she wondered if he had only just remembered the argument they'd had in the woods. "See you later."

What Bethan had been going to say was that they hadn't been in the old history block since they found out that Emily had been dead for weeks. In fact, they had last been there the day before they had found Emily's body. And Emily had been there too.

As she stood alone in the abandoned prefabricated building, Bethan remembered how Emily would appear at the back of the room, her slight frame barely casting a shadow, her thin face sharp-edged and vulnerable.

"I hope you're OK, Emily," Bethan said to the empty room. "I hope you and your mum made it to a nice place, and that you aren't frightened or trapped..."

Bethan's voice trailed off and she glanced quickly over her shoulder. Did something move behind her? Bethan tensed, but she didn't feel frightened. Instead a kind of calm reassuring sensation washed over her. Bethan closed her eyes and as she stood there, something moved behind her lids. Suddenly the acrid scent of burning filled her nostrils. Bethan's eyes flew open, thinking she caught a movement in the corner of her eye. A shadow perhaps, or something reflected in the dirty glass.

"Emily, is that—"

Bethan jumped as the rickety door slammed open and Kelly marched in, looking like she was on battle alert.

"Who you talking to?" she asked looking round at the dingy room. "Your imaginary friend?"

"Sort of. Emily," Bethan confessed. "I miss her."

"I miss her too," Kelly agreed. "I hope she's OK wherever she is, I hope she's not like that girl Tara..." The two were silent for a moment as they remembered that sobbing voice on Jay's digital recorder.

"She's with her mum," Bethan said, "I'm sure she's fine."

Kelly looked Bethan up and down. She was even more dishevelled than usual, her blue hair had faded to a pastel shade and was tangled and unbrushed, and for once she didn't need to pile on the eyeliner to make herself look half dead, as deep shadows bruised beneath her eyes.

"You didn't get any sleep, did you?" Kelly asked.

"Did you?" Bethan replied.

"Not really, but I'm sort of used to that. I can't remember the last time I really slept. But are you OK, after what happened?"

"Am I OK?" Bethan looked puzzled. "I'm fine. Apart from the fact that I'm the new queen of geek. I checked the blog before school this morning and it was jammed up with worse and worse hoaxes, and some just plain nastiness. You were right, I should have kept my head down. If it gets much worse you'll seriously need to think about whether or not you can be seen with me any more."

"Oh, I don't need to think about it," Kelly told her. "I know it's a terrible idea, but I've never been very good at doing what I should."

Bethan smiled. "Apart from that I'm fine. I mean, it's Jay who's got a ghost omen and Charlotte who's cursed."

"I'm talking about the argument," Kelly said. "You and Jay in the woods, before Hashim pulled his stunt and you were on the verge of telling Jay that you like him."

"What?" Bethan exclaimed. "I so was not going to do that, which isn't even true anyway."

"You so were, and don't lie to me. The rest of the school might hate you, but I'm your mate. I know you, I've seen the way you go all soppy over him, and how upset you were about this ghost omen thing."

"You were too, so does that mean you fancy him as well?"

"As well?" Kelly grinned. "So you *do* fancy him."

Bethan dragged her hair across her face. "Oh God, Kelly, shut up." She peered out from between the strands of her hair.

"I..." Bethan looked at the door, Jay would be here any second and this was the last thing she wanted to be talking about when he turned up. "I don't know, maybe... I like him, he's interesting and... oh I hate this." Bethan stamped her foot. "I don't know what to say. I know he's a geek but it's just that he's..."

"Got those killer green eyes that are really intense," Kelly finished for her.

She dropped an arm around Bethan's shoulder. "Jay is improving with age. You like him, Beth. You fancy him, and you know what I think, if someone slapped his head against a brick wall enough times, and I don't mind volunteering, he'd realise he fancies you too. You should tell him how you feel."

"Er, I don't think so!" Bethan huffed, but she didn't bother to deny how she felt any more. "He likes girls like you and Charlotte: flashy and pretty, style and no substance."

"Hey, what are you saying?" Kelly laughed.

"I'm saying that a short, blue-haired Goth is not Jay's type. Everyone knows he's been in love with you since he was about five."

"Was, was in love with me, but I'm fairly sure he's over that now. I haven't caught him doing any of that soppy gazing at me stuff in ages."

"Really?" Bethan sounded hopeful. "But anyway, even if he'd stopped liking you, the last thing he needs right now is some girl crushing on him."

"But you are not some girl, you are *you*. You are his perfect woman, just as mental and geeky and sad as he is. And one of the few people in the world who really knows what he's going through. Maybe you're just what he needs right now." Kelly ruffled Bethan's already messed-up hair.

"Really? Do you think so?" Bethan felt her heart quicken in her chest.

"Why not?" Kelly said. "If we're all going to die, what's the point of waiting? We could all be worm food by the end of term party."

The two girls laughed, and Bethan added thoughtfully, "So if you think we should 'seize the day' does that mean you are going to tell Hashim how you feel about *him*?"

Kelly stiffened and withdrew her arm from around Bethan.

"Yeah, I'll gladly tell him how I feel about him. I'll tell him he's a no-good, low-life, two-faced *coward* who can't even handle a little bit of ghost action and a waste of space too..."

"My ears burning?" Hashim said, appearing in the doorway. "Nice to know you care, Kel."

Bethan watched as Kelly flushed a deep shade of red, turning her back on Hashim to hide her discomfort.

"I didn't think you were coming," Bethan said. Hashim looked worse than she felt, pale and drawn, like he hadn't slept a wink.

"I'm not staying," Hashim said. "I don't want nothing to do with this any more." He stared at Kelly's hunched back. "But I did want to tell you what I saw last night, I think you might need to know."

"Need to know what?" Jay arrived, a little out of breath from running, and dumped his bag on the table.

"The ghost I saw last night, after the séance. The one that scared me... you know, the ghost who spoke to me once..." Hashim swallowed and closed his eyes for a moment. "He was standing behind Charlotte, with his arms crossed across his chest and his eyes rolled right back in his head like a corpse, only he was laughing. Like he thought what was about to happen to Charlotte was funny."

Hashim walked over to Kelly and stood in front of her. "And you know what, Kel, I am a coward. I don't want to face up to any of this crap and I don't care what that makes you think of me."

Hashim clapped Jay on the shoulder. "Good luck, mate. But please, don't ask me to do this again."

Hashim slammed the ill-fitting door behind him as he left, leaving it to slowly creak open again.

"I think that's really it," Jay said. "I think he's really out."

"Only because you didn't tell him about the ghost omen," Bethan pointed out. "If you told him about that you know he'd stick by you until we'd sorted it."

"I wouldn't be so sure about that," Kelly muttered.

"No, he would," Jay said. "But I don't want to make him.

He has to live with bumping into a corpse every time he turns the corner, so he wants to be as normal as he can be. I'm not going to make him go through this just because he's a loyal friend. And you know, maybe I don't have to. Maybe I didn't really see a ghost omen, I mean, if I did where has he been ever since? Like Kelly says, all I have to do is be careful and keep an eye out. Maybe... maybe I don't have to worry."

"Really?" Kelly said. "Only your grandad seemed pretty worried and upset and Bethan *cried...*"

"I didn't cry," Bethan protested. "Do you really think it might be OK, Jay?"

"I'm not going to worry about it any more," Jay shrugged. "I don't want either of you two sticking this out just for me. If you'd rather call it a day and hope for the best, then I get it."

"We'd never leave you," Bethan said, failing to keep the emotion out of her voice.

"Look," added Kelly, "if it was anybody else's ghost omen, I wouldn't be worried. But it's you, Jay. And everyone knows you're a pushover. If you're not going to worry, then neither are we. But one thing's for certain, me and her aren't going anywhere."

"We don't have to do a group hug or anything now, do we?" Jay asked.

"Try it and I'll kick your head in," Kelly promised him.

"OK." Jay unzipped his bag. "First things first, I cleaned up the recording we made last night and put it on the laptop. I played it through from the very beginning. Tara's voice is there at the end... but there's more. Listen."

The girls leant in close to the screen as they watched the sound frequency graphic rise and fall with every word. It was Kelly and Charlotte talking, Charlotte explaining about the séance.

Jay pointed to the screen. "I wasn't sure how best to analyse the recording, so I went online and found this software called Pro-tools. It's used in music recording and stuff like that. It was really expensive, but I found a site I could download it from for free."

"You download illegally?" Kelly gasped in mock horror. "Call the police!"

"Yeah, yeah, anyway. I transferred the recording from the dictaphone into wave files, so that each voice would be represented on screen by a different graphic. See that red line? That's your voice, the blue one is Charlotte's. What else do you see?"

"There's another line, a green one," Bethan pointed out. "But it's really close to Charlotte's voice, isn't it just picking up her too?"

Jay shook his head.

"That's not how it works. This program is designed to create a new graphic for every new voice, so that if you're recording a girl band or something you can produce each voice separately. And besides, if you look closely, you'll see the green line isn't there all the time that Charlotte is talking, it comes and goes."

"What does that mean?" Kelly asked him.

"All it really shows us is that the dictaphone picked up another sound frequency that sometimes followed Charlotte's voice exactly. And it wasn't the same as Tara's files."

Jay fast-forwarded to Tara's voice recording and the three fell silent again, as they listened to the haunting recording, the graphic on the screen convulsing with every sob.

"The recording treats hers like a normal human voice, but this one..." Jay went back to the mysterious green line. "It can't be random, because it's so closely matched to Charlotte's voice patterns – so it's not background electrical interference or anything like that."

"Can we turn it up?" Bethan suggested.

Jay shook his head again. "I tried that, but it's like a really loud whisper. Loud enough for the recorder to pick up, but not loud enough for us to be able to hear it."

"Like a silent scream," Kelly said thoughtfully. The others looked at her. "I don't know about Pro-tools, or wave files, and I haven't got a paranormal blog, like some spangles I could mention, but I think I've worked one thing out. Dead people can make themselves heard without making any noise at all. Whatever that green line is, it's a ghost. And maybe whatever, whoever Charlotte and her friends contacted in the first séance attached itself to each of the girls in turn, like a leech. Maybe that's what it is."

Jay and Bethan both stared at Kelly.

"What?" Kelly demanded.

"That, what you just said. That's really intelligent," Jay said.

"And?" Kelly challenged him. Jay beamed at her.

"Just never realised that you were beautiful and clever, that's all."

"Oi, you," Kelly thumped him lightly on the arm, very conscious of Bethan trying really hard to look like she wasn't bothered. "I have ideas too."

"OK," Bethan interrupted before the flirt fest could go any further. "So, we need to try and work out when this ghost will strike again." She opened her bag and spread out the newspaper reports detailing the deaths of the other girls. "The first one happened on Monday the 21st of the month.

The second, also on the 21st of the next month but on a Sunday. Then Thursday 20th, and the last one also on the 20th, this time a Tuesday..."

"One death a month, that really reminds me of something," Jay said, tapping his fingers on the table.

"It means that Charlotte really hasn't got much longer," Kelly said. "It's the 17th today. If the 'accidents' happen on or around the 20th then she could be in for the high jump any day now."

Bethan pulled what looked like a moth-eaten note-book out of her bag and slipping off the elastic bands that held it together began to thumb through the pages. "My diary," she explained as she checked each date, then paused, flicking backwards and forwards through the pages.

"A full moon!" Bethan exclaimed. "Each of the other Riverbank girls have been killed on a full moon! You know what this means, don't you?"

"That there are werewolves in Woodsville?" Kelly asked.

"No, idiot, it means that we have three days left to save Charlotte Raimi."

Jay stood up, as if he'd just remembered something. "And I think I know who from."

The girls waited.

"For a whole year, he killed once a month and then stopped. Nobody caught him, and nobody knows what happened to him. It's the Woodsville Slasher."

"That's your big reveal?" Kelly scoffed. "I thought we already decided it wasn't him, that the papers were just hyping all that stuff up?"

"We did, but we didn't think of the most obvious and likely thing of all," Jay said. "What if the Slasher only stopped killing because he died? And what if he's been waiting all this time for the chance to get back through and pick up again where he left off? If the ghost of the Woodsville Slasher's been picking off Riverbank girls, then he won't stop at Charlotte. And you know where he'll be looking next."

CHAPTER NINE

It was dark by the time they left the school grounds, even though it wasn't quite six yet. They had talked round and round what they could do to help Charlotte, and still hadn't figured out anything other than a plan to meet at Albert's the next day.

"We should tell her that she's got three days left," Kelly said as they headed out of the school gate, caught up in a ragged crowd of kids from another school. The match must have just finished because the floodlights were still lighting up the pitch. A trail of muddy players and fans, some accompanied by their parents, were on their way home too, the Woodsville kids taunting the latest team to lose to them, undefeated since Hashim rejoined the team.

"Look, I know you don't like her, but surely that's just cruel," Bethan chided.

"I don't think it is," Kelly said. "The poor cow thinks she's going to die any minute. If we tell her it's not for three days, at least she'll know what's what. She can do things that she's always wanted to do, like bungee jump or shave her hair off. I mean you'd like to know, wouldn't you, Jay?"

"Not worrying about it," Jay reminded her firmly. "I think Kelly's right, though, Beth. We have to tell her."

Bethan tried to imagine what it would feel like to find out you only had a few days left to live. Who was she to tell someone that everything, *everything* was going to end on the next full moon?

"Maybe there isn't anything we can do," Kelly said thoughtfully, dragging the ends of her coat around her. "We have no idea how we're going to send an evil ghost back to hell, or wherever it came from. What if there's nothing we can do about any of it? And if one ghost can get through and hurt people, what's to stop more and more of them coming? How are we gonna tackle that?"

The three of them stopped, crowds of kids and parents still milling past them.

Jay with his hair messed up, coat hanging off of one

shoulder; Bethan with her black bitten fingernails and blue hair; and Kelly, twisting the gold sovereign ring that belonged to Sean, and which she always wore on her thumb. They looked like a sorry collection of nobodies who couldn't fight their way out of a wet paper bag, never mind save the world. And in that second it hit home.

"Are we sure that we haven't got this wrong?" Kelly voiced what they were all thinking. "Are we sure we haven't got a case of, you know – mass mentalism or whatever?"

"Hysteria," Jay said quietly.

"Yeah, I mean look at us. Our normal lives are pretty dull and dead-end. Maybe we just needed something to think about, apart from either getting a job at the car plant when we leave school or going on benefits..."

But as she spoke, silence fell over the playground. The shouting, screaming kids were still rushing by, but their wide mouths, running feet and dragging bags made no noise, as if someone had just pressed mute on a remote. The sun, which had been steadily sinking below the skyline, seemed to be extinguished in an instant and it was suddenly night.

And there they were. The ghost army. Standing perfectly still amongst the crowds of living pushing past them; the living totally unaware of the horror that vibrated just beneath the surface all the time, all around them. The dead seemed to be staring at Kelly, Jay and Bethan, with the gaping holes where their eyes had been. Waiting for them to give in, give up – waiting for surrender.

"We might be just some kids off the estate, but that's not all we are," Jay managed to speak, raising his voice. "I'm a Romero. This is my destiny."

The army seemed to waver, flicker for a moment.

"And I'm not going to let any dead person push me around." Kelly tried to sound as threatening as she possibly could. She nodded at Beth, who floundered, trying to think of some declaration.

"And I... have the power of knowledge to defeat evil!"

Kelly laughed, and distracted by the flash of her teeth, Jay smiled. And in that moment the army was gone, the noise and chaos of the world around them rushed back in and they could breathe again.

"You laughed!" Bethan looked mortified.

"*The power of knowledge*," Kelly giggled. "Beth, was that all you could think of?"

"It worked, didn't it?" Bethan said. She tried not to show it, but she was genuinely stung. It was all right for everyone else: Kelly the warrior and Hashim the ghost whisperer. Even Jay had his destiny and his ghost omen. She was the only one who didn't have anything special and it sucked.

"It did work," Jay said, and began walking again. "And I think I know why. When we're together, we're stronger. We're not afraid, we give each other courage and that gives us power."

Kelly and Bethan had to trot to keep up with him.

"This isn't mass hysteria, and we haven't made it up. But if we all stick together, then maybe we can beat them. We can push them back to where they belong because we have each other and for some reason, the four of us together are..."

"Invincible?" Kelly suggested.

"Maybe strong enough," Jay said.

"Which means two things," Kelly countered. "It would seriously affect our chances if any of us die and..."

"We need Hashim," Bethan finished for her.

Just at that moment someone called out Hashim's name, and looking up, Kelly saw him jogging across the street to catch up with a teammate.

"I'm going to talk to him," she said.

"No, don't!" Jay grabbed her arm. "Don't, Kelly, he asked us not to."

"Jay, you just said we're strong when we are together... if we're gonna have a chance we need him."

"Do not tell him about me," Jay warned her.

"Fine," Kelly sighed. "I won't tell him about you. But

seriously, we need him. Without him, we're just a Goth, a ginger geek and me."

"Why don't you have an insulting nickname?" Bethan asked her.

"I'd have thought that was obvious," Kelly replied sarcastically. "I've got to talk to him. He'll listen to me."

"Kels, just don't... let him upset you," Bethan tried to warn her, but Kelly was already marching across the road towards where Hashim had just said goodbye to his mate.

"I'll see you at Albert's," she called over her shoulder as she went.

Bethan and Jay looked awkwardly at each other. Since that fight over nothing very much in the woods, the balance of their friendship had changed. And now it seemed like she had to think really carefully about everything she said, or the way she looked at him, or even what she wore when she knew she was going to see him.

"So are you walking back then?" she asked hopefully.

Jay stuffed his hands in his pockets and stared hard at his toes.

"Actually, I was thinking I might um... go this way," he nodded in the opposite direction from the estate. "There's this thing I have to do, over there... so. Better go, don't want to be late... for the... thing. Anyway, see you."

Jay turned sharply on his heel and headed off into the twilight.

"Bye then," Bethan said miserably. Kelly had it so wrong if she thought Jay liked her. She sighed, taking one last look at Kelly walking quickly beside Hashim, gesturing like she was trying to make a point, and then began to trudge home.

"But you can't just walk out on this!" Kelly repeated, even though Hashim was doing his best to ignore her, walking fast as he headed for home, iPod plugged in, head down. "They're everywhere – all the time, just waiting for their chance. Hashim! Don't ignore me!" In desperation, Kelly yanked hard on the wire, pulling the earphones out of his ears, but also ejecting the iPod out of his pocket at the same time, so that it clattered to the floor, and skidded a few feet along the cracked and dirty pavement.

"What the...?" Hashim bent down and scooped it up. "What are you trying to do, Kelly?"

"I'm trying to make you see that you're part of this," Kelly cried exasperated.

"No, I'm not," Hashim said. "I never asked to be part of anything. Just leave me alone!"

"How can you think that this has nothing to do with you,

when you're the only one who can really do anything? This has *everything* to do with you. It's your life!"

"Who says?" Hashim asked her. "I didn't ask for this to happen to me. I'm not the one with the destiny. This, it's like... like Jordan Finch, getting asthma for the first time last year. For a bit he thought it'd change his life, that he'd get kicked off the squad – but they sorted him out with an inhaler, and now he plays better than ever."

"There isn't an inhaler for ghosts, Hashim," Kelly said. "Please, I... We need you. They're coming for you too."

"I don't care," Hashim said.

"You do, I know you do. I know the reason that you are so shaken and upset by what happened to Emily and Tara and those other girls is that you do care, you care a lot."

They stopped, and for second stood looking into each other's eyes.

"You're wrong," Hashim said. "I don't care, I am a coward, I just want an easy life. Leave me alone!"

"No!" Kelly said as Hashim began walking again. "Hashim, I can't leave you alone."

"WHY NOT?" Hashim turned, shouting in her face, shocking Kelly into a stunned silence. "Go on, Kelly, explain why you won't quit torturing me."

"I..." Kelly caught her breath, closing her eyes. She wasn't about to say what she was going to say, was she?

"*I* need you," she told him softly, almost in a whisper, forcing her lids to open so that she could look him in the eye. "Before, I thought you and me... I thought something was going on, and I wouldn't never had said anything but... it made me happy, being with you." Tentatively Kelly rested one hand on Hashim's arm, feeling a thousand times more frightened than she had facing an army of ghosts. "You felt that too, didn't you?"

Hashim bit his lip and looked right into her eyes. "No. No, Kelly, I didn't."

Neither one of them moved for what seemed like ages, and it was only when Kelly felt the chill of a tear tracking down her face that she turned away and began walking back towards the estate, going a few steps and then pausing.

"I'm sorry I embarrassed you, yeah?" she said, her voice raw, unable to turn and face him. "Please, don't talk about this to anyone."

"Kelly..." Hashim spoke her name so quietly that she almost didn't hear him. She waited, unable to bring herself to look round at him. "Nothing, whatever..."

"Whatever," Kelly said, and she kept walking until she was certain that he wouldn't be able to see her any more.

The hole in Jay's trainer meant that, by the time he'd completed his large loop of the streets surrounding the estate just so that he didn't actually have to walk home alone with Bethan, his sock was completely soggy and wet, squelching uncomfortably inside his shoe. There was something seriously off about Beth, and not just that she'd started to be the one who knew stuff, who looked things up. Ever since they'd started to spend time together, he'd thought she was funny and clever, but recently, instead of their friendship settling into something that Jay understood, Bethan seemed more... well, more like a girl again. Always talking and fluttering her eyelids. Jay found this new Bethan much harder to talk to. Besides, he needed to get away and get some space. He needed time to think without two bossy girls yacking on in either ear. He'd told Kelly and Bethan that he'd decided not to worry about his ghost omen any more, but that was a lie. He just didn't want them to think about it every minute that he spent with them, because when everyone was thinking that way it was almost like being dead already.

Having cold and wet feet didn't exactly help when it

came to focusing his mind. Jay sighed, kicking at and missing a discarded balled-up crisp packet that skittered across his path. He'd been on at his mum to give him some cash to get some new clothes and stuff for ages. He knew money was tight at home, but he couldn't help it that he'd grown so much recently, shooting up another couple of inches and broadening out across his shoulders so rapidly that his bones ached. He could roll up the sleeves of his shirt to hide the fact that the arms were too short and wear it unbuttoned over a T-shirt because it didn't do up any more, but there was nothing he could do to detract from the fact that his trousers stopped centimetres above his ankles or that his supermarket trainers were falling to pieces. It was hard enough being the ginger geek in the cut-price clothes, but being the ginger geek in the cut-price clothes that didn't fit was almost too much. Jay stopped in his tracks. *How ironic*, he thought, that his body was bursting with so much life, exploding in all directions, dragging him into adulthood, but what for? Any day now all of that energy and effort would be cut short, cut down. Finished. And it didn't even look like he'd get to go out in style. Forcing himself to start walking again, Jay smiled ruefully. Kelly would never love him back at this rate.

Kelly King was still just as wild and as beautiful and

intermittently scary as she always had been, but the way he felt about her had changed. Before, she was this unobtainable girl, a mythical creature safely out of his reach. Now, she was part of his life, she cared about him – she cared about everything – even if she did her best to hide it most of the time. It was pretty obvious even to Jay that she had a thing for Hashim, but even so... The crush he'd had on her for years and years had ebbed away as he'd got to know her, but in its place now was something more real. And when she realised that nothing was going to happen with Hashim then he'd be there, waiting for her. Or at least, he hoped so. Jay stopped abruptly and looked around. His out-of-the-way route had led him back into a part of the estate that he didn't recognise.

When the estate was built, all four corners of the massive sprawl had been designed to be identical, symmetrical. But over the years, each quarter, dominated by its own tower block, had evolved its own identity. Jay's corner was probably no less dark and dingy than this one, but it was familiar dark dinginess, with broken street lights and abandoned shopping trolleys splayed on their backs that he greeted like friendly landmarks signalling that he was almost home. A haven for criminals: what with the gangs, the crime, the drugs and almost total absence of police. But when a place was your home, even if all those things were going on around you, you sort of got used to it. And whatever the reality was, life in the flats never seemed quite so dark or dangerous as outsiders saw it. For Jay it was his sanctuary.

Being in a part of the estate that he didn't know was a bit like wandering into a parallel universe, Jay thought, desperately wishing he could wander into a new universe round about now.

The square courtyard, enclosed on either side by covered walkways, was surprisingly empty for this time of the evening. Usually there'd be kids from school, hanging out on bikes or boards, girls in groups pushing each other around, laughing, talking to or texting the person they were standing next to. But this place was totally empty. There wasn't even the muted sound of bass vibrating somewhere or some deaf old lady's telly turned up to full volume. Jay stopped in the middle of the square and looked up, trying to get his bearings. He wasn't worried, he could see the tops of the four towers from here, each one bristling with satellite dishes and mobile phone masts. He knew he'd find his way home eventually, it was just that he didn't want to spend all night doing it, not with wet, cold feet and the exhaustion of yesterday's sleepless night creeping up on him.

He'd walked around the park after he'd left Bethan, turning left and left again at the end of every street he walked down, knowing that eventually he'd hit the estate. He should be on the corner vertically opposite to his own now, so if he walked straight on towards the central concourse it should take him less than fifteen minutes to get home, take his shoes and socks off and warm his feet in front of the electric fire, while Mum cooked his tea.

The thought was such a comforting one that for a second Jay didn't notice a figure in the shadows just a few metres ahead of him. The second Jay realised he wasn't alone, he halted, his heart pounding, blood rushing through his veins. Instantly Jay knew the figure was waiting for him, and more than that, he felt something that he hadn't felt in weeks. Like a part of him that had been missing had returned.

It was his ghost omen; the other Jay.

As he walked towards his own ghost, the strangest feelings, or rather anti-feelings washed over him. It was like he was suddenly made of air, that he was light as a feather and that with each step he took, a gust of wind might easily sweep him away and drop him somewhere, out in the deepening night. Jay's feet didn't feel cold or wet any more; in fact, he didn't feel anything at all. He was just his mind, his soul – he wasn't sure what, but somehow the only part left of him was his essence. For a few moments it felt like he'd been loosed from the prison of his body, like he was the ghost omen and the ghost omen was him.

Then his double stepped out of the shadows and Jay's heart started pounding against his chest.

"You're back," Jay said.

The ghost omen nodded, his image seeming to solidify as Jay stared at him, the near full moon gilding his translucent skin in silver light. His other, dead self, looked exactly like him, except whatever it was that animated this strange being, it wasn't life. Jay forced himself to look at his own death. The black sticky blood was everywhere, soaking his shirt from his neck down to his waist... although he couldn't see a wound. That was when Jay noticed something he hadn't seen the first time. Dead Jay was wearing a checked shirt, and even in the poor light and when it was covered in blood, Jay could see quite clearly that he was wearing a red checked shirt. But Jay didn't own a red checked shirt.

Jay swallowed, struggling to drag what courage he could find out of his gut and forcing himself to speak.

"I don't suppose that you're me after I accidentally discover the secret of time travel and that I've just decided to become rebellious and break the prime directive and alter history? Like in *Star Trek*? Have you heard of *Star Trek*? Of course you have... You're me." Jay trailed off. "Or maybe you've just wandered here through a hole in the space-time continuum and need my help getting you back to your own universe? Because that would be cool, it'd be like an episode from *Dr Who*. We like *Dr Who*."

"I wish I was," Jay's ghost replied. It was like hearing his own voice recorded on an answerphone or video – it sounded like him, but different.

"So, I do die then," Jay said. Strangely he didn't feel the fear he expected to, or any kind of terror. Only an odd peacefulness, like running into a long-lost friend. Perhaps it was his body going into shock, protecting his heart and brain from exploding by making the whole thing seem like a dream. *It's a bit like when I had that injection before they took my back teeth out*, Jay thought absently.

"The first time I came to you," Ghost Jay said, "that time when you ran away, it had only just happened. I wasn't really sure what was going on myself. When your brain is dying, it invents ways of protecting you. All I knew was that I had a message I had to give to you. When I came to you, I didn't know I was... we were dead, not till later. I've been trying to come back ever since, but it can be... difficult."

For an instant, Ghost Jay seemed to tremble and shiver,

like the reflection on the surface of still water that had been broken by a stone.

Jay swallowed and looked at himself, wearing the black and red checked shirt, his hands still covered in black, dried blood.

"Is it the army of the dead? Can you tell me more about them, what they want? What they are going to do?"

Ghost Jay shook his head. "It's not like that here, if there's a plan I don't know what it is. It's just... chaos and anger and fear."

"No fluffy clouds or endless peace?" Jay asked himself.

"Not here." Ghost Jay looked around him. "We don't have much time."

"Well, look, tell me what happens," Jay said hopefully. "And then I can change it. I don't care if it's the prime directive. I mean, when did Kirk ever bother about that, right? If it's a matter of life and death, even Spock's prepared to bend the rules."

"I can't," Ghost Jay replied. "I want to, but I don't really know. Most of the time it's just a string of images that don't make any sense. Sometimes I get pulled back to that moment, the moment we die. I can hear a girl screaming and see blood and there's pain... I feel everything as if it's happening again, and then I am nowhere. Like this sort of grey empty nothing. I don't know if I'm there for seconds, hours or decades, or a million years, but time doesn't matter, Jay, they always come for you in the end."

"The army?" Jay asked anxiously.

Ghost Jay didn't answer. He was looking around him as if he expected unpleasant company, very soon.

"I don't understand," Jay went on, hurriedly. "There has to be something, someone controlling what's happening, trapping souls, but who? Why? Jay?"

"I don't have a lot of time..." Ghost Jay's voice had faded, it was thinner, weaker.

"Well, warn me then!" Jay pressed him, as fear began to creep in around his numbed edges. "Surely, the point of you meeting me is so I can do something to stop it, to stop myself – us – from getting killed and ending up like you!"

Ghost Jay shook his head sadly. "We're dead. At some point in your future, it's already happened. It's still happening in that moment, over and over again, and it always will. Jay, you can't change time. Our death is a fixed point. It must happen, but not the others. We *can* save the others."

Jay's ghost looked round sharply, then stepped back into the shadows. "I don't want to go with them."

Jay heard the plaintive whispered words echoing all

around him. His ghost, his own dead self was terrified of what was waiting for him in the afterlife. Jay felt sick, caught in a dream that he couldn't wake up from, knowing he was going to die, knowing there was nothing he could do to stop it. And almost worse, that once it had happened he'd be lonely, frightened and powerless.

"There's got to be *something* I can do," Jay said. "I've got to be able to save myself from this."

"You can save her life, if you listen," Ghost Jay whispered urgently. "Look for the looking glass. Put right what is wrong and... what's precious must be lost, for the truth to be found."

"What?" Jay exclaimed. "A sodding riddle? I'm going to die and have my spirit imprisoned by an army of mean ghosts for all eternity and the best you can do is give me a riddle?"

Galvanised by desperation, Jay stormed towards the shadows to confront himself, but before he could, he was repelled violently backwards by a freezing force-field of dark energy. As Jay fell backwards he saw himself, crouching down, exposed by the street light, his arms folded over his head.

"No! No, I don't want to go with you, please!" His own voice that was not his voice rang out, verging on a scream.

Pushing himself up on to his elbows, Jay stared in horror as his ghost appeared to be dragged down, down through the thick concrete, down into the cold, clammy, root-bound earth. The last part of him that Jay saw was his ghostly fingers, clawing uselessly against the concrete paving slabs.

Alone again, Jay realised that his lungs were burning, it felt as if he hadn't drawn breath for the whole time he'd been talking to his ghost omen. He almost had to force himself to gasp in a ragged breath, the fresh air burning his chest. A wave of nausea swept over him, and he collapsed face first on the ground, feeling something sharp sting and graze his cheek. Jay rested his face on the rough, cold concrete, pressing his cheek into its reassuringly solid surface, and cried.

He was going to die, he was going to die and there would be no big tunnel, no white light waiting to take him to heaven. There would be only darkness and cruelty and fear, and he didn't want to go. He didn't want to go.

"Oi, gay-boy." Jay started, footsteps clattering towards him at speed. He recognised that voice from somewhere.

"Is he dead?" another younger voice asked.

"Out of it on something, probably, see what he's got on him."

Jay sat up abruptly, and looked round. Four boys; a couple a bit older than him, two a bit younger. The voice he recognised was the kid who'd been hanging outside his grandad's the other day. The one who'd given him the speed.

"You been crying?" One of the younger boys peered at him.

"What's wrong, boyfriend dumped you?" another one taunted in a sing-song voice.

"Hey, it's you, the ginger geek I fixed up." The big kid tipped his head on to one side and took a couple of steps towards where Jay was sitting. "You owe me a tenner, mate."

Slowly Jay got to his feet. He didn't know when he was going to die and he didn't know how. But Jay knew one thing; it wasn't going to be now. Because right now, as usual, he was wearing his brilliant old, ripped, too tight, over-washed school shirt, with the biro stain on the pocket. Suddenly it became a magical garment that meant he didn't have to be scared of anything or anyone. Nothing, Jay realised, as he dusted grit from his palms, nothing could touch him.

"Get out of my way," Jay told the kid.

"I don't think so," he said. "I want my money. If you

haven't got it, I'll take what you have: phone and cash. If you're lucky, we might let you go."

Jay smiled, and reached into his pocket to draw out the small plastic bag that was still there. He threw it at the kid, and it bounced off of his shoulder and split on the floor.

"I didn't want it in the first place," Jay said.

Jay didn't flinch when the kid pulled a knife.

"Get him," the kid instructed two of the smaller lads. Jay let the younger ones grab his arms.

"Go on then," Jay said, nodding at the knife, and then made the youngest boy jump by suddenly laughing. "Have you ever stabbed anyone before?" Jay asked him. "Do you know what it feels like, pushing a blade through skin and flesh? Would you have the guts to look me in the eye? You got to get up close, you know, you've got to get right in the face..."

And without warning, Jay ran at the kid, who clearly saw something in Jay's face that he'd never seen before. He dropped his knife, turned on his heel and ran, cohorts following close on his heels.

Jay stood in the centre of the empty square, mad adrenalin fizzing in his veins. He tipped back his head and laughed, enjoying every tiny sensation of being alive: from the blood whooshing in his ears to the bite of the tiny pieces of glass that had embedded themselves in his cheek. Jay didn't know how long he had left to live, who did? But between now and... and that frightened ghost that he was destined to become, he wasn't going to leave *anything* undone.

Kicking the knife down a drain, Jay began to run home, not because he was scared, but because he wanted to feel his heart pumping, his lungs burning, his legs aching. He wanted to feel as alive as he possibly could for every single second that he had left.

CHAPTER TEN

"Are you OK, Jay?" Kelly asked him as he jogged along beside her on the way to the lift. He'd turned up at her front door first thing that morning. Kelly had been mortified, grabbing her stuff and attempting to usher him out of the door before her dad heard a male voice in the flat and dragged his carcass out of bed to see what was going on.

"I just thought it'd be nice to walk you to school," Jay said with a disarmingly sweet smile, the intensity in his voice making Kelly pause and look at him for a moment. His green eyes seemed very vivid this morning, but there was something else different about him that she couldn't quite put her finger on. "I thought we could talk."

Kelly looked sideways at him and frowned. "Really? I

was sort of going to school with Yana and Bea this morning. Yana's birthday is coming up and she's having a party on Friday. We're gonna talk about who's wearing what, who's going to snog who... you know, Jay. Girl stuff."

"Yeah but, we've only got thirty-six hours until the next full moon – actually probably less – because three out of the four girls who died, copped it in daylight – so I'm thinking we really have to sort this out before sunrise tomorrow."

"I can still get twenty minutes off to walk to school with my mates, can't I?" she insisted a little testily as they waited for the lift to rumble its way up to meet them. "Stop staring at me, man!" she told Jay who had leant against the wall and gazed at her. "You're fully freaking me out."

"Can't help it." Jay smiled at her again. "You're really beautiful, Kel."

"Shut it, you mental," Kelly told him mildly, as the lift pinged to signal its arrival, but she couldn't help smiling as they stepped inside the small steel cubicle. She liked this new, slightly-mad bolder boy that had turned up at her doorstep.

"We should bunk off after registration and meet up then," Kelly said. "You and Beth can maybe walk to school together and talk about... things."

"Bethan does seem to be having all of the ideas at the

moment," Jay observed, as he watched Kelly's profile. "It's a good job one of us is."

"There's more to Bethan than ideas, you know," Kelly said pointedly.

Jay shook his head and chuckled at the way Kelly's temper would flare at the slightest spark. He hadn't really slept last night and he suspected that he probably never would again. Why would he want to miss any of the waking moments left in his short life? Everything seemed different, as if someone had come and wiped a damp cloth across everything, removing all the grit and grime to reveal colours that were brighter, smells that were sharper, sounds that he had never noticed before; like his mum boiling the kettle that morning, thundering in his ears. He'd watched her, half asleep, the buttons on her cardigan done up wrong, buttering his toast with too much butter, like she always did. Jay loved his mum, the same way that anybody does, a sort of background affection that persists no matter what. But that morning as she absently ruffled his hair when she handed him his toast, Jay had felt an explosion of emotion in his chest. Mum would take it really hard when he was gone.

"I love you, Mum," Jay had told her, hugging her hard before he went out.

"What have you done?" his mum asked him, gently teasing.

"Nothing, I just wanted to tell you that I love you. You're a cool mum."

"You want those new trainers, don't you?" his mum smiled. "You always did know how to pull my heartstrings, right from the day you were born."

The lift juddered to a halt on the ground floor and Jay followed Kelly out into the brisk chill of a Woodsville spring morning.

Bethan was hovering on the concourse, her long black skirt tangled round her ankles, her blue hair whipped across her face by the wind, and a short distance behind Yana and Bea were making their way over to greet Kelly. The moment Bethan caught sight of her friends she began walking, almost running to meet them, clutching a battered bit of paper in her hand.

"You went to call for Kelly?" Bethan asked Jay.

"I was up early," Jay shrugged.

"Oh. Right." Bethan didn't ask why he didn't call for her when they lived in the same tower, a few floors apart.

"Coming, Kels?" Yana and Bea arrived at their little group. "Or are you lot planning your next chess tournament or something?"

"Funny," Bethan smiled tightly, turning back to Kelly. "Anyway I did it. I Googled Charlotte Raimi and I found out something pretty interesting."

"I Googled it and I found out like I have a face like an arse," Yana mimicked Bethan cruelly. "Seriously Kel, come on."

"Hang on, don't speak about me like—" started Bethan.

"Like what?" Yana pushed her. "What you going to do about it, freak? Look it up on the internet?" She pushed Bethan again, harder with every word. "I'll. Push. You. Around. As. Much. As. I. like. Because. You. Are. Nothing."

On the last word she shoved Bethan so hard that she fell to the floor.

"Hey, lay off her." Jay knelt down beside Bethan, putting himself between her and the other girls.

"What a freakshow," Yana shook her head. "Let's go."

"You shouldn't have done that," Kelly said quietly, staring at the toes of her boots.

"What, picked on your little special-needs mate?"

"Yana, I'm not going to make it to your party," Kelly said, looking up, her eyes full of summer lightning.

"Why not?" Yana said. "Because you're choosing that waste of space over me?"

"No, because I'm fairly sure you aren't going to want the person who gave you a black eye to be there." And then Kelly hit Yana in the face. She doubled up in pain, howling, clutching her hand to her cheek.

"You cow!" she wailed. "You cow! I'm going to... I'm going to..."

"Trust me," Kelly told her as she picked up her bag, "whatever you've got, I've seen worse."

The three walked away, and no one spoke for a good ten minutes. They were almost at school by the time Bethan piped up.

"Do you want to see what I found out on Google?" Bethan struggled to flatten out the piece of paper, clutching as it fluttered and twisted in the breeze. "I thought Raimi didn't sound like a common name, so I searched that and Boston first. I got like a million hits, so then I searched *Charlotte* Raimi, Boston and I found a photo of her at the launch of her dad's new business, about a year ago. That didn't tell me much except that the family had only recently moved to the city. So *then* I searched Charlotte Raimi, Massachusetts and I got this! A story from *The Salem Evening News*, from about eighteen months ago. Listen:

"LOCAL GIRL REVIVES TOWN WITCHCRAFT PAST WITH HIGH SCHOOL COVEN."

"You *what*?" Kelly said, snatching the paper out of Bethan's hand and reading out loud – "Scandal rocked Salem High School for Girls last night, when it was discovered that a coven of teen witches led by the daughter of prominent local family, the Raimis, had developed at the school. Charlotte Raimi, aged fourteen, had recruited thirteen of her classmates to follow her own obsession with the so-called cult of Wiccan and the 'craze' quickly spread through the school. Girls were encouraged to concoct love potions and even throw curses on less popular pupils, culminating in an attempt to evoke the spirits of the dead through... *séances!* The lying little cow!" Kelly spat. "It was her, she knew about the whole open/closed pentagram thing and the plants and the crystals all along – she knew exactly what she was doing! I *told* you!"

"Let me see that." Jay took the piece of paper out of Kelly's hand and read on. "Several of the girls that had become involved in the coven became ill, stopped eating or talking – until one girl finally broke down and confessed to her family, echoing the horrors of the infamous Salem Witch Trials of 1692, in which residents were hanged after being accused of witchcraft by two local teenage girls. Although Miss Raimi has committed no criminal offence she has been summarily expelled by the school, and it is believed that several of the parents of the other girls involved are filing law suits against the Raimis, citing the psychological damage done to their children." Jay shook his head. "No wonder the family had to move out of town. And if Charlotte kept dabbling in all that stuff that'll be why they sent her to Riverbank. Big mistake. They had no idea they were sending her to ghost capital of the world," Jay finished.

"OK, so now that we know that I was right ALL ALONG, and that Charlotte Raimi is a horrible, two-faced lying actual witch," Kelly said, "instead of risking our lives to try and save hers, can we just forget it?"

Jay frowned. "We've still got to find a way to stop the Woodsville Slasher spooking around, offing anyone who takes his fancy. Whether she meant to or not, Charlotte opened up a portal. We need to do everything we can to send the Slasher back and plug that hole up again. Even if it's only a drop in the ocean of darkness that's coming, if it slows it down for just one day, then it's worth it."

Bethan and Kelly stopped across the road from school and looked at Jay.

"What's happened?" Bethan asked him, her face grave.

"I saw my ghost omen again," Jay told them, struggling to say the words out loud. "He... he told me that being dead isn't any fun, and being dead in Woodsville is... well, you heard Tara's message. It's a frightening, lonely, endless nightmare. He couldn't tell me when it would happen or how, only that there was no way of stopping it."

"Well, don't take his word for it," Kelly said brashly, but with a small high voice. "Jay Romero's always getting things wrong."

"Oh Jay," Bethan reached out to him, but Jay sidestepped her touch, afraid her kindness would break his resolve not to show how frightened he was.

"It's cool, it's fine. I'm dealing with it. The ghost, he was wearing a shirt that I don't even own – one that I would never, ever buy, actually – that means it can't be soon. So while I'm here, we do everything we can to find out what's going on and turn it back. And when I'm gone, you two can't stop until it's done, OK? Promise me. Don't leave me in that place alone."

"You're not going anywhere," Kelly said firmly, kicking the pavement with the toe of her boot. Yana was walking past holding one hand over her eye.

"We promise," Bethan said steadily. "Jay... we'll need Hashim. You'll have to talk to him, tell him what's going on."

"Bethan's right, we need all the help we can get and he's

180

the only one of us with the bona fide special powers," Kelly said painfully. "There's no point in me talking to him, but he'll listen to you, Jay. You have to talk to him. Today."

Jay nodded. "OK, I will... but let's not do the whole doom and gloom thing. At least I know when it's not going to happen."

Jay stepped out into the road, causing a bus to screech to a grinding halt to avoid running him down and only narrowly avoiding being flattened by a speeding Astra travelling in the opposite direction. Horrified, Kelly and Bethan hurried over the road to join him as soon as it was safe.

"What are you *doing*?" Kelly demanded furiously.

"No shirt," Jay said, pulling out the frayed collar of his greying school shirt. "I'm not getting run over today." He grinned. "You know what, knowing you are going to die is actually quite liberating."

Kelly nodded across the road to where Charlotte Raimi was standing. She looked terrible, her sleek blonde hair tangled and dirty, her eyes wild and wide. She barely looked like herself.

"The full moon," were the first words that came out of Charlotte's mouth as she confronted them. "Tara, Lucy, Jade and Denise – they all died on the day of a full moon. And that's tomorrow."

"How did you find out?" Bethan asked.

"I looked in my diary— you mean, you knew already? I haven't seen or heard from you since that awful séance. And you've known this since then? Some help you are!"

"Hang on," Kelly said. "We might have made quite a lot more progress if you'd bothered to mention in the first place that you're a witch!"

"What?" Charlotte demanded, her cheeks flushed and her eyes glittering with fear. "How... how did you know?"

"We Googled you, *obviously,*" Kelly said. "Any more lies you'd like to tell us?"

Charlotte buried her head in her hands, tangling her fingers in her hair. "I never meant for this to happen. It was only supposed to be some fun!"

"I don't think Tara and your other mates are finding it very funny, do you?" Bethan challenged her. "Why lie, Charlotte? What else are you hiding?"

"Nothing," Charlotte said, her face drenched in tears. "I'm not hiding anything. I just didn't want it to be true. I didn't want it to be my fault they died. There is no one, no one else who can help except all of you. I didn't want you to hate me, if you hated me then you would never have helped me."

"Not true, actually," Kelly said. "I hated you at first sight."

A steady stream of kids were pushing past them now, making their way into school, some stopping to stare at Charlotte.

"Look, you can't stay here," Bethan said. "We need to go in and get registered. Wait for us in that café on the precinct that we met you in the first time, remember?"

Charlotte nodded.

"As soon as we can get away, we'll be there. And don't worry. We want to find a way to stop this just as much as you do. This isn't just about you." Bethan looked at Jay. "It's about much more than that."

Kelly was complaining as the three of them walked, a little late, into class for registration. "Seriously, if that girl wasn't going to almost certainly die a horrible death tomorrow, I'd slap her up good... Jay! What?"

Jay was staring at her again.

"You," Jay said. "You."

"Me what? What's your—" But before she could finish her sentence, Jay took her in his arms and kissed her. Right there in front of everyone. Jay had never kissed a girl in his life, although he'd imagined doing it to Kelly time and time again. And now it was happening, his lips smashed against hers, resistant at first and then, miraculously, she kissed him back, her arms winding around his neck. Jay felt a million different emotions going off like fireworks inside of him, but mainly a happiness that was so pure and complete that he felt as if he might float away with Kelly in his arms.

"Romero! What do you think you are doing?" Mr Bacon thundered as he stormed into class. "Put that girl down now!"

But it seemed like neither Jay nor Kelly heard him.

"I said, put that girl down." Finally Jay released Kelly to the claps and jeers of the others. Kelly stood there, speechless, staring at Jay as if she had never seen him before in her life.

"I've always wanted to kiss you," he told her. "Since we were about five."

The class and Mr Bacon waited with bated breath for Kelly King to rip Jay Romero's head off.

"Yeah?" Kelly managed to say when she finally caught her breath. She looked around at the expectant faces of the others and then caught Bethan's expression. She was standing in the doorway, hurt pulling at every corner of her face.

"Tell me honestly," Jay said, his mouth curling into a smile. "That was a good kiss, wasn't it?" Kelly could feel Bethan staring at her but she knew that what she said now would either make or break Jay. She'd explain to Bethan later.

"Best kiss I've ever had. They say it's always the quiet ones!" Kelly said winking at the class. Everybody cheered and Mr Bacon slammed his folder down on his desktop as hard as he could.

"That's it. King, Romero, detention for both of you!"

"Not me, sir," Jay said. "I won't be here. I fancy a day off. Oh, and I didn't do that homework either. See you later!"

Everyone watched open mouthed as Jay strolled out of class.

"ROMERO, GET BACK HERE NOW!" Bacon yelled.

"Hey, sir?" Kelly said. "Has anyone ever kissed *you*?"

"Well, what did you expect me to say?" Kelly said to Bethan who was marching off ahead of her, as she tried to catch up in her heeled boots. They had stayed for registration and then snuck out through the fire door next to the girls' changing rooms on the way to games. Bethan hadn't spoken a word to Kelly the whole time. "Beth! Can you imagine what it took for him to do that in front of everyone, I couldn't just diss him, could I?"

Kelly didn't add that actually Jay's kiss *was* the best kiss she'd ever had. For the first few seconds she'd been too shocked to do anything, and then by the time she realised what was happening and that technically she should be punching his lights out she realised that she rather liked being kissed. It had been exciting, and it made her wonder what it would be like to kiss someone who she really cared about. If Jay's kisses could make her feel that way, then imagine what it would be like kissing Hashim.

"Come on, you can't be mad at me. It wasn't my fault."

Bethan sighed and slowed down a little, allowing Kelly to walk at her side.

"I know," she said. "I know it wasn't your fault, it's just... Kelly, the first boy I've ever liked not only likes another girl but he's... he's going to die a probably horrible death and then have to endure a terrible afterlife. I mean, it's not fair, is it? It's the definition of not fair, right?"

Kelly slung her arm around Bethan and squeezed her. "What's so good about normal teenage life, anyway? All you do is spend all day worrying about stuff that you can't change or control and trying to look like you don't care. Before this I didn't have any real friends, everyone was scared of me, no one ever..."

Kelly had been about to say "kissed me" but thought better of it. "...really knew me. You spent most of your time hanging out on your own, dyeing your hair and trying to talk your mum into letting you pierce bits of you."

"Why us, though?" Bethan said, plaintively. "Why not

Carrie White or Yana and her mates, why aren't they the ones lumbered with saving the world from an army of ghosts?"

"Are you joking? Carrie White couldn't swat a fly. I don't know why we got lumbered with all this destiny crap, but we did. And now we've just to get on with it."

"How, though, how are we going to do anything without Jay?"

"He's not gone yet, Beth," Kelly said.

"Jay said there's nothing anyone can do to stop it."

"Yeah, well, like I said before, what does Jay know about anything?"

CHAPTER ELEVEN

When Bethan and Kelly caught up with Jay in the café, Charlotte was cowering in the corner. Jay was leaning across the table, talking to her in a low voice, which seemed to be calming Charlotte down.

"Look," Jay said as Kelly and Bethan sat down, completely normally as if he hadn't just recently snogged the face off one of them, "Charlotte and I have talked and there's nothing else that she's hiding. She started mucking about with the witch stuff to get her parents' attention, but she didn't plan on getting sent away to Riverbank, and she definitely didn't plan for the séance to go the way it did. She never believed for a second that anything she did would work, it was just a way of making friends in a new place and a new country. She has to live with knowing that what she started ended up in four of her friends dying."

"Not for very long..." Kelly had muttered under her breath.

"*So* before we do anything else, we have to be clear that we are going to lay off Charlotte, OK? I had an idea while I was waiting for you, so I nipped into the library on the way here. There's this local history website, you'd love it, Beth. It's got everything that's ever happened in the Woodsville area, going back centuries. Whatever's happening at Riverbank has got to be to do with the place itself, about something that's happened there before. That's probably why there was a Ouija board in the attic in the first place, because other people have tried to find out what could be going on there too. So I thought I'd see if I could find something, anything that might give us a clue, and found these pages on Rupert Godfrey, lord of the manor." He produced a bundle of paper from his bag. "I haven't had a proper chance to look at them yet, but I printed out as much as I could."

Bethan took the ream of paper off Jay, trying not to notice the way he smiled at Kelly. By the time they arrived at Albert's place, she'd managed to read most of what Jay had found and she couldn't believe her eyes.

Charlotte looked distinctly uncomfortable as she stood in Albert's living room and Bethan got the impression that she was doing her best not to wrinkle her nose at the sour smell that always seemed to inhabit his flat. Meeting Albert for the first time was always a shock for anyone, with his long hair, eyepatch and stumps instead of legs. He wasn't exactly your typical grandad.

Albert had listened while Jay and the others filled him in on what had happened at Riverbank two nights ago and then Jay played him the recording and showed him the mystery wave file on his laptop. He explained how they'd worked out that the other four deaths happened on a full moon, once a month.

"And we're pretty sure the ghost that's come through is the Woodsville Slasher," Jay finished.

Albert shook his head. "Not the Slasher. No, won't be the Slasher, the Slasher is what it is not."

Charlotte frowned, pulling her mouth down. "Is he funny in the head?" she whispered to Bethan loud enough for all of them to hear, including Albert.

"I assure you, I've got my marbles, love," Albert told her.

"Lovely to meet you!" Charlotte nodded and shouted, as if she were talking to a deaf person.

"Well… we really think it is, Grandad," Jay went on, a little deflated. "One death, once a month, just like the Slasher – no one knows why he stopped killing. The most obvious explanation is that he died. Maybe he's been waiting for a chance to come back and start killing again."

"It's a good theory, son, don't get me wrong,' Albert said. "But it's not the ghost of the Slasher this young lady contacted. Woodsville Slasher isn't dead, you see."

"What?" Kelly gasped. "You mean, he's actually started murdering again?"

"No, I mean that this has got nothing to do with him." Albert slipped out his top teeth and ran his tongue over his gums before popping them back in.

"But…" Kelly looked dumbfounded. "Albert, no offence, but this thing with Jay – it's shaken you up. You've been upset – are you sure that you're right about this, because… we worked it out and everything."

"I'm as sure about that as I am about anything," Albert said.

"So how do you know that it's not the Woodsville Slasher?" Kelly asked him. Albert looked uncomfortable.

"I just know," he said. "If I could tell you about it I would, but I can't. Just take it from me, the murderer is alive and well, and if he'd killed anybody recently, I'd know about it. There are some things the coppers can't deal with, love," Albert told Kelly sternly, as if that should be the end of the matter.

"All those children killed and he's never paid the price for it," Kelly said. "He's like an evil psycho, roaming around making cups of tea and watching telly!"

"Um, I think Albert's right, you know," Bethan suddenly said. "I think we might just have found out who our ghost is... it all fits!"

"Tell us then," Jay said. He had been so certain about the Woodsville Slasher that all this came as something of a shock, and it rankled him a bit that after he'd collected the research on Riverbank it was Bethan that got to do the big reveal.

Kelly privately fumed for reasons of her own. Even if she had to do it on her own, she was going to found out who the Woodsville Slasher was and make sure he got what was coming to him.

"It's all here." Bethan held up a sheet of printed paper. "It says back in the mid-seventeenth century, the lord of Riverbank Manor wasn't only the local squire, he was the local magistrate too."

"Yeah, we know," Jay said. "Hanged a load of people and buried them in the woods; Charlotte told us. Most of them were..." He looked around at the others. It had been staring them in the face all along, "...*witches*."

"It says here that most of them simply had the misfortune to be a bit eccentric or different," Bethan said primly, before reading on. "Those were turbulent times, the country torn apart by civil war, family fighting family, it was mostly a lawless land. And some unscrupulous people, Godfrey being one of them, used the fear and uncertainty to their own advantage."

She looked up from the page. "Because back then people believed in witchcraft, it was real to them and they were scared to death by it. A wave of witch-hunts swept across the country. In the space of a year, five hundred people were either burnt or hanged for being a witch."

"Eighteen innocent people were hanged in the woods behind the school," Kelly said quietly. "Now that's the sort of reason for angry haunting that I get."

"Well, most of them were probably innocent – but there was one woman, who really did practise Wiccan art, wasn't there, Charlotte?" Bethan looked at the Riverbank girl, who had become very quiet and still. "And I've got a feeling that you know all about her."

After a moment Charlotte began to talk in a quiet resigned voice, perfectly calm as if she were discussing a turn for the worse in the weather.

"Her name was Rebecca Morris," she told them in a flat

monotone. "They said she put a curse on the crops, killed off their livestock and made their children sickly and weak. But all she ever tried to do was help them. They wouldn't leave her alone, they tormented her, bullied her – tried to hound her out of her home. They forced her to turn to the dark arts. And as they put the rope around her neck, she cursed them all, every one of them present, their children, their children's children for generations to come."

"Brilliant," Kelly said. "Nothing I like better than a curse from beyond the grave."

Charlotte ignored the interruption. "Rebecca stood there and looked everyone present in the eye, and the witnesses said it felt like she was looking into their souls, and then she cried out, 'All here...'"

"Cursed with death," Jay finished. "Exactly the same as your first message through the Ouija board."

"You were *trying* to contact a witch?" Bethan asked Charlotte. "I thought you said no more lies?"

Charlotte shook her head as tears filled her eyes. "No, I didn't know about her, not before. We all knew the history of the house, it's in the welcome brochure. But the school is very careful not to tell the girls anything that might unsettle or upset them. I had no idea about the hangings or Rebecca until after the séance, and then... I just, seemed to know."

Charlotte caught Kelly scrutinising her closely. "I swear to you, that's the truth!"

"So the séance allowed Rebecca to come back and continue wreaking her revenge," Jay said, "and this time she doesn't mind who she attacks."

"Not quite," Bethan said. "There are a lot of local names here: the people who were there when the curse was first issued. A couple of them rang a bell, so I checked against the newspaper articles about the Riverbank deaths..." Bethan looked a bit sheepish, "...that I keep in my 'Weirdsville' ring-binder. Anyway, Charlotte's friends were from local families; families that have lived in this area for hundreds of years. Some moved away briefly, Tara's family had even lived overseas before coming back – that's got to be more than a coincidence, hasn't it?

"I think," Bethan continued carefully. "I think that all four of the girls who died were distant relatives of people who were present at Rebecca's hanging."

"That's what I call persistence," Kelly said. "She must have been a Capricorn, this Rebecca Morris."

"Hang on." A thought dawned on Bethan. "If Rebecca's that persistent then, well, there must be hundreds, maybe even thousands of relatives of the people who hanged her living in Woodsville today – she won't just stop at five!"

"Or four hopefully," Jay added tactfully, glancing sideways at Charlotte, who had her head bowed, her hands folded in her lap.

"But Charlotte's safe – she's from America," Kelly said. "There's no way that she could be related to anyone who was in Woodsville four hundred years ago."

"I wouldn't go that far yet," Albert said. "If it was this young lady who contacted Rebecca, and knew enough about witchcraft to attract her spirit from wherever it had been languishing, then I'd say Charlotte is central to everything that has been happening. I wouldn't say that makes her safe."

Suddenly Charlotte laughed loudly, making everyone turn and stare at her. She clapped a hand over her mouth. "I'm so sorry, I don't know why I just laughed... it's just I suddenly got a picture of us sitting in this flat at the top of a skyscraper, in this little stinky kitchen talking about witches and ghosts and I thought it was funny."

"Mental much?" Kelly commented rolling her eyes.

"There is one other thing you need to know, Jay," Bethan said, so seriously that she instantly had everyone's attention, including Charlotte's.

"The eyewitness account I've been telling you about? The man that wrote it was dead inside a month, and four of his five children too: the plague caught them. Only one, tended to by a local wise woman, survived it and went on to have children of his own. His name was Nathaniel Romero."

Suddenly what Bethan was saying hit Jay hard in the face. "He gave me a warning, though, and there was nothing about witches."

"Who gave you a warning? You've seen your ghost omen again, haven't you?" Albert asked him, his one good eye watery and bloodshot. Jay nodded and told his grandad about his second meeting with Ghost Jay.

"There's nothing I can do, Grandad. Nothing at all. But I don't have the red checked shirt yet... Maybe Rebecca's ghost is after me, but that doesn't mean she's going to get me, does it?"

Slowly Albert nodded, pressing the back of his gnarly hand against his mouth as he steadied himself. "We can be prepared. Rebecca's ghost is just as dangerous to you as she is to Charlotte. It's more important that you send her back before sunrise tomorrow than ever. And there's only one way to do that. You need someone more powerful than she is."

"You mean like a priest? Where are we going to find a priest who is going to listen to us, believe us and then come up to Riverbank and sort out a ghost?" Kelly scoffed.

"You don't need a priest," Albert told her. "What you need is a person who possesses spiritual power, who lives with one foot in the world of the living and one foot in the world of the dead. You need..."

"Hashim," Kelly said, the realisation weighing her down. She'd never felt like this before, wanting to see someone so badly and dreading seeing them at exactly the same time.

"But what if we can't get Hashim back?" Bethan said.

"What do you mean?" Albert asked, concerned.

"He doesn't want to be part of this any more," Jay told Albert. "He wants his life back like it used to be."

"I can see why," Albert said. "But for some people that is not a choice they get to make. You need him there tonight, if you are to have any chance at all. Think about it, Jay, Rebecca doesn't just want you, she wants your mum, your dad, your cousins in Birmingham, me. Once she's started she won't stop. You need to make Hashim understand."

"But I don't want to be the person who drags him back to all this... horror," Jay said unhappily.

"Like I said, Jay," Albert said so sadly. "Sometimes you don't get a choice. You know that, son."

Before they parted, they arranged to meet Charlotte at the school that night, in the same place and at the same time, around ten. Any earlier and the teachers would still be up, any later and they might not have enough time to deal with the ghost before midnight and the next full-moon day emerged.

"What can we do while you're seeing Hashim?" Bethan asked. "There's got to be something we can do to help."

"Well, ghost or not, we're dealing with a witch. You know a bit about it, Bethan, see what more you can find out – ways of protecting us and holding her back. Even if it's all hokum and it doesn't work, Rebecca will take it seriously."

"What about me?" Kelly asked him. Jay looked at her for a long time, a slow smile spreading across his face.

"Kelly, you are the most beautiful, brave, funny girl that I know," Jay told her.

"Oh well, um." Kelly looked at Bethan, who dipped her head and tucked her hands under her arms. "That's not true, you know Bethan too."

"Yeah, Bethan's cool too, but I just wanted to say that..."

"Jay, just because you are going to die it doesn't mean you can develop social Tourette's," Kelly warned him.

"But kissing you made me realise something," Jay said "I'm not actually in love with you, after all."

Bethan's head snapped up.

"Oh... right." Kelly wasn't sure how to react to that.

"You are one of my best friends, though," Jay added. "You and Beth both are and I want you to know how glad I am that I've had friends as good as you." Jay turned his gaze to Beth, who bit back the threat of tears by chewing hard on her lip. "You're both really, really cool."

"Oh, so having a crush on me is a waste of time now, is it? Why don't you just give me a paper cut and squeeze lemon juice in," Kelly said, desperate to make light of a moment that was becoming unbearably sad.

"I'm just saying," Jay said. "I'm not as much of an idiot as you think I am, OK?"

Jay stopped at home on his way to Hashim's. His mum would be back from work, cooking tea for Dad, and she'd worry if he didn't let her know that he wasn't going to be back at the usual time. Someone from school might have been in touch about his absence today, but if he was lucky his parents still wouldn't know. Jay's mum and dad were the only two people left in the universe who didn't own a mobile phone or an answering machine.

Jay could have called his mum, of course, but he wanted to see her. On what might be his last day alive, he wasn't ashamed to admit that he wanted to see his mum.

"Hello love," Jay's mum said, as he walked in and dumped

his school bag on the kitchen floor. He put his arms around her and hugged her tight, wondering when he had grown taller than her – he hadn't noticed before.

"Oh now, stop that," she chuckled. "You don't have to try and butter me up any more, you've got your way."

"Have I?" Jay said. "What way is that?"

"I've been putting a bit aside and I picked you up some new bits in the market today."

She nodded at two blue plastic bags that sat on the table in the next room. Jay stood stock-still and stared at them, that tearing feeling inside ripping a little wider apart. He didn't have to look to know what was inside the bags.

"I was going to make you wait until payday, but well, you were lovely this morning and when do you ever get a treat?" She nodded at the bag. "Go on then, tell me what you think!" His mum gave him a gentle shove towards the table.

With the distinct feeling that his heart had stopped beating, Jay opened the first bag. Inside were a brand-new pair of trainers that looked almost exactly like Nikes.

"Brilliant," Jay said, taking them out and turning them over in his hands. "Thanks Mum."

"Look in the other bag," she said. "There's a couple school shirts, but there was this stall that had a three for two thing on and I thought, you seem to be spending a lot of time with girls these days, so you could do with some glad rags."

"Glad rags," Jay repeated. First he lifted a grey T-shirt with a print of an old American car on the front of it, then a plain black shirt. And then folded neatly in the bottom of the bag, the price tag still attached, sat his destiny, in the form of a red and black checked shirt.

"The man behind the stall said it was all the rage now, do you like it?"

Jay dragged his eyes away from the shirt and looked at his mum as his heart plummeted.

"Amazing, I've done something right for once!" she beamed at him.

"Yes, Mum," Jay said, kissing her on the cheek. "More right than you know."

CHAPTER TWELVE

*H*ashim was having a difficult time trying to kill some zombie monsters that would only die if you shot them with their own crossbows, which was tricky because you had to kill one in the first place to get a crossbow. He sighed as he got killed for about the ninth time in a row and threw down the controller. It didn't help that there was a new ghost sitting on the chair in the corner of his bedroom. There'd never, ever been a ghost in his bedroom before, and until he started having the nightmares it had been the one place where he'd felt safe.

Not that this ghost, a woman who Hashim had never seen before, who had shown up a few days before, was that scary. She didn't talk, she didn't do anything, she wasn't even frightening. She just sat and watched him as if she were waiting for something, something that Hashim could not work out.

He was trying his best not to look at her, working on the basis that if he ignored her she'd go away. But the ghost just sat there gazing at him, not with anger or fear – in fact there was something surprisingly comforting about her presence – but still, Hashim wanted her to go. He wanted all of them to go and for just a few minutes his head to be clear of the constant wordless whispering that chattered on and on every moment that he was awake and most of the time he was asleep too.

There was a quick tap on his bedroom door; both Hashim and the ghost looked up as Jay poked his head around the corner. Hashim didn't want to notice that the ghost smiled, but he did. She had a lovely smile.

"What do you want?" he growled at Jay. At that precise moment there was only one alive person in the world who he wanted to see less than Jay, and that was Kelly. Hashim had just been walking into the classroom when he caught Jay kissing Kelly. He'd stood there a few steps away from the doorway as Kelly told the whole class what a great kisser Jay was. In an instant he'd felt like someone had punched him in the stomach, and he was swallowed up in the strangest feeling that he couldn't get his head round. He couldn't like

Kelly. He couldn't be with a girl who was so deep in with everything that was going on around him, because if he did then he'd never get away from it. That was why he couldn't tell Kelly that he liked her, and ask her out on a date and do the things that normal people did. But it didn't mean that it was OK for anyone else to be with her.

And now Jay was here in his bedroom and it seemed like the ghost was pleased to see him.

"I know you don't want to see me," Jay said.

"You still came, though." Hashim picked up his games controller again and stared at the screen, his hands going through the motions, even though he wasn't really seeing it. "So what are you doing here?"

"I didn't want to come but... I haven't got any choice," Jay said. "Hashim, we need you. *I* need you. Something's happened, or it's going to happen – the point is, I'm going to die, quite probably tonight."

Hashim listened to everything that Jay had to say in silence, his eyes fixed on the TV screen, watching his onscreen character die over and over again. As Jay talked, the ghost seemed to be listening intently, nodding every now and again, and Hashim got the feeling that he was being drawn back into a nightmare.

"And my grandad said that sometimes we don't have a choice. Sometimes we just have to do something, because it's our destiny. You have a choice. You don't have to help me or Bethan and Kelly, but I don't. I had to come here to ask you. And there's something else..."

Hashim waited.

"The ghost omen told me that Bethan and Kelly are in danger too, that I couldn't be saved, but that if I heeded his warning I might be able to save them."

"His warning?" Hashim said, still staring ahead.

"He said to look for the looking glass, right what is wrong, and what's most precious must be lost for the truth to be found."

"You *what*?"

Hashim glanced up from the screen and looked the ghost in the eye for the first time. Her expression was etched with fear, her beautiful dark eyes brimming with tears.

"Exactly," Jay said. "Apparently there's nothing in the ghost omen manual that says you have to make sense. Anyway mate, like I said, it's your choice..."

"No, it isn't. I don't have a choice," Hashim said slowly. And as soon as he spoke the words out loud, the sense of entrapment that had been dogging him over the last few weeks fell away. "Everywhere I look, and I mean everywhere,

I see dead people. And it doesn't matter how much I try and escape from them, they always follow me." The woman in red smiled bravely at him, nodding in encouragement, and he smiled ever so slightly back, taking strength from her. "Ever since Emily, I thought this ghost thing was a curse, that it was trapping me, dragging me down into a life I didn't want. I've been trying to run and hide. Pushing everything and everyone who's involved with it away from me. But I think I've just realised: denying it is what's driving me mad."

Hashim looked at the woman Jay couldn't see. "And I think that's what you've come to tell me, isn't it?"

She nodded, and then before Hashim's eyes she faded, the colour draining from her face, her beauty and radiance decaying. Suddenly shadows crowded round her, long dark fingers that seemed to entwine her in their grasp.

"Can't you talk? Isn't there anything you can tell me?" Hashim asked. He gasped as in an instant the beautiful woman was dragged through the wall, every trace of her comforting presence disappearing in the same moment.

But she had left something behind. Jay came to stand beside Hashim as they stared. On the bedroom wall, scratched into the paint were two words. "Help her."

"Emily's warning," Jay breathed.

Hashim ran his fingers through his hair, every particle of his body jangling with adrenalin and a sense of purpose. "So this ghost version of you said there was no chance for you, that no one or nothing could save you, yeah?"

Jay nodded, bleakly.

"Yeah well," Hashim squared his shoulders, "I'm not like anyone else. I talk and ghosts listen, ghosts get scared. So I don't care what this omen says about what is going to happen to you, mate. Nothing he said counts any more. Not now I'm back on board."

Hashim and Jay looked at each other for a second and then, ever so briefly, they hugged.

"So," Hashim said, feeling for the first time in months that he was himself again. "Show me where this ghost is – I'll zap it."

Jay had only meant to pretend to go to bed while he waited for his parents to fall asleep in front of the telly with the lights off, like they always did on a Friday night. But it seemed that his vow to never sleep again was one he couldn't keep and he must have drifted off as soon as he crawled under his duvet. A text from Kelly woke him saying that she and Beth were already waiting at the bus stop on the high road. Scrambling out of bed, bleary-eyed and still full of sleep, Jay reached out for the clothes he'd taken off earlier and dumped on his chair. He pulled the shirt on over his head without undoing the buttons and yanked on some tracksuit bottoms that were lying on the floor.

Jay slipped his feet into his old trainers. Cold wet feet were the least of his worries, and at least this way his mum could get a refund on the new ones. Weirdly, considering that tonight was certainly going to be the most deadly and dangerous night that he had ever spent, he felt calm, cheerful even. For the first time ever in his short life Jay felt he was really living. He'd been bold, fearless, confident, rebellious. If this is what facing death did for a person, then Jay supposed it wasn't such a bad thing – except for the death part. He crept out of the front door to the sound of his parents' stereo snoring and made his way off to meet the others. He was a Romero, this was his destiny.

It was as Jay approached them – Bethan and Kelly standing together, Hashim waiting slightly apart – that he reached up to scratch the itch that had been irritating the back of his neck ever since he'd left home. His fingers stumbled across something hard-edged, a bit of cardboard. With a yank, Jay pulled a label from its thin plastic tag. He came to a stop under a street light and unzipped his coat. His mum must have come into his bedroom after he'd dropped off and left his new clothes on the chair. Without even realising it, he'd put on the red and black checked shirt.

The others all stared at him as he pulled his shirt-front out and held it under the street light.

"God, Jay," Kelly said. "It's tonight."

CHAP✝ER THIRTEEN

The empty hallways of Riverbank Girls' School echoed with their footsteps as they followed Charlotte down the wood-panelled corridors, dusty portraits of people long gone, seeming to peer at them as they went by.

"What I don't get," Kelly said, unable to resist the urge to break the silence, "is why there aren't more ghosts here? This house is four hundred years old. How many people must have died here? Not to mention those poor people who got hanged out there." She nodded through a long, diamond-paned window at the shadow of the forest. It loomed against the night sky, almost as if it were gathering, preparing to march under the light of a nearly full moon. "Why did it take a bunch of schoolgirl witches and a Ouija board to start something?"

Kelly looked at Hashim, who had been avoiding eye contact with her since they'd met at the bus stop. The last thing she wanted was to have to talk to him and pretend like everything was OK. But he wasn't getting off the hook that easily either, just because he turned up to save the world. Again.

"Do you see any ghosts?"

Hashim looked around and then shook his head. "I'm not even getting a spooky feeling."

"Well, that doesn't mean much," Jay reminded them. "If anything that's a bad sign." Jay was still feeling surprisingly calm and cheerful. Charlotte seemed pretty happy too, the anxious careworn girl they had seen that morning was gone. She had an air of excitement about her, a sparkle in her eyes, like a little girl on Christmas Eve. Perhaps Charlotte felt like him, perhaps it was because the moment was finally here. There wasn't any time left to be frightened or fearful.

"I think there are fewer ghosts because of the woods," Bethan said as Charlotte led them, not up the narrow dusty staircase but onwards to a turret at one corner of the mansion and then up a stone spiral staircase.

"Like I said before, the trees used to act like a... like a spider's web, catching all the spirits that tried to escape and keeping the ghost world where it was supposed to be.

Riverbank is one of the few places left in Woodsville that is still hemmed in by trees. I think Charlotte tore a hole in the web with her Ouija board and that's how Rebecca Morris came through." Bethan looked at Jay. "I know you think I'm completely off the wall..."

"No, I don't actually," Jay said. "I assumed you must be wrong because Grandad had never said anything like that. But I've only just realised, there are millions of things he hasn't told me. A billion things I don't know. Everything you say makes sense, Beth. And when this is over, we'll go and talk to him about it, together, because I'm sure he will agree with you."

The trouble was, both of them thought silently as Charlotte pushed open the door to her dorm room, there was very little chance that both of them would still be alive in the morning.

"What are we doing here?" Jay asked, stepping into the large circular room, in which none of the furniture fitted properly. There were two sets of bunk beds pushed up against a curved wall and one single bed that jutted out awkwardly towards the centre of the room. In between the beds there were three sets of drawers and one dressing table, with a large mirror propped up haphazardly against the wall, an assortment of make-up and jewellery jumbled across its surface. For some reason a metal-framed chair was propped up against it, tipped upside down so that its tubular legs reached towards the ceiling. One large long sash window, that was open halfway, let in enough moonlight to make electric light unnecessary. "Shouldn't we be up in the attic?"

"The health and safety people were up there today, while I was with you at your grandfather's flat. They ruled it unsafe – the floorboards are riddled with rot – so they've taped up the doors to make sure no one goes in there until it's fixed. I thought our... my room would be as good as any. This is where all five of us slept, a lot of the girls' things are still here. I thought it might help."

Bethan looked sceptical.

"Jay, this afternoon," she said. "I've been finding out more about witchcraft and I think the reason that Rebecca has struck during the day of a full moon is because it's this moon, just on the brink of becoming full, that is supposed to give witches the most power. It's even called the Witches' Moon."

Jay looked at Charlotte who was standing by the door.

"Did you know about this? Is that why you've brought us here, because of the Witches' Moon?" he asked. She leant back against the wall, tipping her head to one side so that her tangle of blonde hair fell over one shoulder.

"Yes, I did know about the moon. Look, she's coming here tonight whether we like it or not. I just wanted to give us the best possible chance of fighting her—"

"And how is this helping?" Kelly asked, as she advanced on Charlotte. "You were there, weren't you, at Albert's place? You did hear him say that Jay was at the top of witchy's wish-list for grisly murder? If you do anything, anything at all that makes this worse for him then you won't have time to worry what Rebecca's going to do to you, because I will have already ripped your head off, got it?"

Charlotte didn't even waver under Kelly's stare. Instead she just smiled slightly, holding her gaze.

"If you'll let me finish, we can trap the power of the moon and use it against her... all we need is a mirror." Kelly backed away uncertainly and looked at Bethan.

"That's right," Bethan said quickly. "There's so much witch folklore around, it's hard to know what's what, but there is one legend that says a mirror can be used to trap the moonlight and contain its power until it's broken again." She looked at Charlotte. "That is possibly quite a good idea."

"We should try it," said Jay. Secretly, he was remembering his cryptic warning: *look out for the looking glass*. If Bethan was right, then the mirror could help protect them.

Together Hashim and Bethan lifted up the mirror that

was propped up against the dressing table, knocking some nail scissors, a metal file and pot of red nail varnish on to the wooden floor, some of the thick red liquid snaking out of the bottle neck as the lid came loose.

The only place where the mirror could directly reflect the image of the moon was leant against the door, blocking the only exit. But if it would rob the witch of her power then it was worth the risk.

"What about the board? Is it still in the attic?" Bethan asked. Charlotte shook her head.

"I knew the inspectors were going up there so I brought it down last night, just in case..." She nodded at the alcove of the dressing table behind the upturned chair, that appeared to be filled with books, shoe boxes, and all sorts of junk. "It scares me, so I put it under as much stuff as possible and that chair in front of it, silly really."

Jay slid the upside-down chair out of the way and dug through the piles of stuff until he found the board, looking quite small and innocuous. "We should put it in the middle of the room, I guess," he said.

"Wait." Charlotte stepped forward and pushed the single bed to the side, freeing the corner of a rug that covered the middle of the floor. Yanking it aside, she revealed a pentagram, painted in red directly on to the floorboards.

"You did that specially?" Kelly asked her suspiciously.

"Ages ago, even before we found the board. Just messing around, you know."

"But it's open," Bethan said. "There's no protective circle."

"Which is why I was just about to chalk around it!" Charlotte produced a piece of chalk from her pocket, and kneeling began to close the pentagram. No one noticed that as she crawled around the floor making the circle, the trailing edge of her foot simultaneously rubbed one arc of the circle out.

Bethan looked at her watch. "It's gone eleven, we're running out of time."

They looked at each other, full of apprehension and uncertainty.

"What do we do now?" Kelly asked.

Jay looked at Hashim.

"Remember what Grandad said?"

Hashim nodded.

"Good luck, mate," he said to Jay.

"Jay—" Bethan began, but he stopped her.

"Everything's different now that Hashim's here. If you've got something to say to me then say it tomorrow. I'll buy you a coffee and we'll talk, OK?"

Bethan bit her lip. "OK."

All eyes turned to Hashim, who stood, poised and strong, waiting. There was a glow about him, a light that seemed to kindle in his eyes, a glowing ember, just a tiny spark waiting for one deep breath to ignite it. Hashim looked at his friends to steady himself, feeling for the first time what they could see. A power that he barely understood, pulsing inside of him.

"She's here, waiting. I can feel her, she's really strong, but I can't see her. I don't know why I can't see her."

He took a breath and held out his arms, palms facing up.

"Rebecca Morris, come forward. Step in the pentagram and show yourself."

There was silence in the room, even the spring breeze that had been blowing through the window dropped. Kelly held her breath and waited.

"Rebecca Morris, make yourself known, show yourself to me!" Hashim commanded with a little more authority.

"Nothing," Jay said after a few seconds of silence.

"But she's here," Hashim insisted. "I can feel her, almost as if she's standing next to me."

"Um..." Bethan's eyes widened, and her throat suddenly went dry as she whispered, "I think she *is* standing next to you."

Bethan rose a trembling arm and pointed at Charlotte. She was hanging in mid-air a few inches off of the ground. Her body was limp, her arms flopping at her sides and her head lolling over. But her eyes were very much alive. And they were fixed on Hashim.

"Charlotte's possessed," Jay gasped, his fascination keeping his terror momentarily at bay. "That's why she's been acting like two different people, she *is* two different people. Sometimes Charlotte, sometimes Rebecca – that's why there were two wave files on the tape."

"Rebecca Morris," Hashim spoke to the eyes that burnt out of Charlotte's limp body, "I command you to step into the pentagram."

Laughter tore from Charlotte's throat, her mouth working, forming words that belonged to another, older voice.

"You silly little fool," Rebecca's voice rasped and wheezed. "Why would I do anything you tell me to when everything here is placed just so? The mirror doesn't trap a witch's power, child. It doubles it. There is nothing a mere boy can do against me." Charlotte's mouth, flecked with spittle, twisted into a grotesque smile. "Only two here are cursed by me, but all of you must die. I have been commanded to see that you join the ranks of the dead by sunrise."

Hashim stood firm. "I am no boy, witch. I am Hashim

Malik, destroyer of evil. I have power that you can only guess at. You will do my bidding or be crushed forever into the darkness from which nothing may return!"

A piercing screech ripped from Charlotte's throat and before Hashim could move her body flew at him, like a horrifying puppet. She smashed into Hashim, propelling him backwards until he slammed against the mirror, which shattered into hundreds of sharp shards, dumping his cut and bruised body hard on to the ground.

Jay stood rooted to the spot. He should be doing something, he knew, but all he could hear were the words of Ghost Jay's warning going round and round in his head. He could hear them, but he couldn't act. This was it. This was the moment of his death and he was going to meet it like a coward.

"Hashim!" Kelly leapt to his side but the witch blocked her way, dragging her off her feet by the hair, as Kelly screamed and kicked. And then in slow motion, Jay saw everything clearly. *Right what is wrong.* The chair, the metal chair with its legs sticking up in the air, like four blades, just waiting...

"No!" Kelly screamed as she was flung backwards towards the upturned chair, which Jay kicked out from beneath her a split second before she landed, hard on her spine.

Look for the looking glass. Jay turned back to see that Charlotte had grabbed a shard of broken mirror, blood from where it cut into her hands running down her wrists as she lunged at Hashim.

Hashim held out a palm and seemed to halt her in mid-air, before she could descend on him, his whole body shaking with the effort to hold her back. "Be gone from this girl, be gone from what is not yours, be gone from this place, be gone!" Hashim kept talking as he clambered to his feet, pushing Charlotte back inch by painful inch. As they struggled, Jay glimpsed Charlotte's terrified face, fighting with Rebecca's spirit, her tormented face twisting and contorting as Hashim fought on.

"Your curse means nothing to me," Hashim told her, as he seemed to gather strength. "You have no power over me. I am *your* curse. I am *your* end."

Without warning Charlotte turned and flew at Jay. In the confusion, he felt her nails clawing at his neck, her hands in his hair as she latched on to him and beat his head, again and again against the corner of the dressing table. This is it, Jay thought dimly through the pain, as he fought the black tide that swam around the edges of his vision. Dying really hurts.

"No!" Bethan shrieked, leaping on to Charlotte's back,

dragging her down to the ground with every ounce of strength she could muster. Kelly grabbed Charlotte's legs and between them, they pinned her to the ground as Hashim spoke over her. Charlotte's body rocked and shook, twisting violently with each word.

"I return you to the darkness, I bind you there, in the blackness, time without end, where you shall always remain."

One last buckle of her body sent Bethan shooting backwards, slamming against Jay. As if from a distance Jay saw the ghost of the witch, torn from Charlotte's limp body, her furious face full of hatred as she launched herself at Bethan. Half blinded by the blood that was stinging his eyes, without knowing how he could do it, only that he must, Jay grabbed Bethan around the waist, twisting round and falling on top of her, shielding her from the witch's onslaught with his body.

"Be gone witch, be gone and tell the others – don't mess with Hashim Malik, I don't take no prisoners!"

The silent scream vibrated within all of them, shaking every single cell of their bodies to the point of disintegration. And then, it was gone, and the only sound was of Charlotte sobbing, face down on the floor lying in the very centre of the pentagram.

Broken, battered and bruised, Kelly clambered up, tasting blood on her lips.

"Jay!" she screamed, seeing him sprawled over Bethan, a dark patch of thick blood drying, matting the back of his hair. "Hashim, help me!"

She scrambled across the floor to get to him, and between them, Kelly and Hashim pulled Jay off Bethan. His shirt and hands were covered in blood, but his face was like marble, white as if every drop had been drained out of him.

"No!" Kelly sobbed. "No, Jay, no, no, no..." She laid her head on his bloody shirt and wept, feeling Hashim's hand rest on her shoulder.

"I'm sorry, Kel, I really am," he whispered.

"God, my head is killing me," Jay moaned. Kelly sat up a little and looked at Jay whose forehead was wrinkled in agony.

"Is he a ghost?" she asked Hashim.

"I hope not," Jay moaned. "I hope being dead doesn't hurt this much, and I feel sick. I'm going to be sick..."

"You're alive!" Kelly yelped, hugging Jay so hard that he almost passed out again.

"Not for much longer if you keep hugging him like that, Kel." Hashim knelt beside Jay and put his hand on his shoulder. "You made it, mate. You made it!"

"I think we need to call an ambulance." Charlotte's thin voice could just be heard.

"Yeah, she's right. He might have brain damage or something, although I'm not sure how we'd tell," Kelly said, grinning at Jay.

"No," Charlotte said, her voice so small and frightened that it made Kelly look up at her. "It's Bethan, I think she might be dead."

Kelly and Hashim turned round to look at Bethan. She was lying perfectly still, with fixed eyes staring up at the ceiling, a dark pool of blood spreading out under her head, like a halo, and a shard of broken mirror jutting out of her neck.

EPILOGUE

Kelly slipped her hand into Jay's and squeezed it. A week had gone by since that night at Riverbank. Jay had been kept in hospital for four days. He still looked pale though and he had to take a lot of pills to deaden the pain.

The doctor had told him that two, maybe three blows more and he would have been dead. He *should* have been dead, but he wasn't. Bethan had saved his life.

"Look out for the looking glass," Jay repeated as Kelly rested her head on his shoulder, Hashim sat on the other side of her as they waited. Bethan's parents were sitting on the far side of the room. Mrs Carpenter hadn't stopped crying since it happened and from time to time Bethan's dad would look over at the three of them, as if he knew who to blame.

"The looking glass, well that was obvious. I should have seen that it was a warning, not advice. But I wasn't thinking clearly..."

"None of us were thinking clearly," Hashim said.

"Some of us didn't even know about the warning," Kelly added, but not in an angry way. When she'd discovered how Jay had protected her and Bethan, despite everything he was going through, she felt something that could only be described as her heart bursting with love. Not that kind of love – but the sort that her life had been all too empty of before.

"Right what is wrong, the upside-down chair nearly killed you, Kelly," Jay said. Kelly nodded, she didn't like to think about how close she had come to being impaled on a chair.

"And what's precious must be lost for the truth to be found," Jay finished. "What did that mean?"

"Maybe it's something you haven't looked for yet," Charlotte said. The three looked at her. She'd come today because she felt she had to before she was flown back to Boston. Within minutes of dialling 999 the ambulance had turned up at the school, and with it the police – to a bloody scene of mayhem. Bethan and Jay had been whisked away to hospital immediately, but Hashim and Kelly were left there with Charlotte to try and explain. Charlotte took all of the blame.

She told the police how obsessed she was with witchcraft, how she'd seen Bethan's blog and couldn't resist trying to wind them up.

"It was such a stupid blog, and they were all obviously so gullible. It's so boring here," Charlotte said. "A girl's got to make her own entertainment."

Charlotte explained how she had sneaked the others into the school after tricking them into believing there was a real ghost there. She told them it was a prank gone wrong. She'd set up loads of tricks to frighten them, but they worked too well. Jay slipped and bashed his head on the table corner, and then slipped again every time he tried to get up, and so bashing himself repeatedly. In her fear, Bethan tried to get away, but fell on to the broken mirror although none of them were sure how the mirror had got smashed in the mayhem.

It seemed like Police Inspector Torrance didn't truly believe what she was saying, but as they all backed up Charlotte's story and there was no evidence of any drugs or alcohol he had no choice but to believe them. Charlotte's mum flew over from Boston and in the end, all that happened was that Charlotte was expelled from another school and sent back to America. The four deaths of the Riverbank girls were put down to tragic accidents soon after.

"Maybe it's the part of the warning that hasn't come true

yet, the part of the warning that is for me?" Jay wondered out loud.

"Typical Jay," Kelly said, quietly. "Why couldn't you have told us what's what, and actually be useful for once?"

"That wasn't me yet," Jay said. "This is still me."

Jay looked down at his legs, not quite able to believe that he was still alive. He was so certain that he was going to die that night. Was he the first person in history to beat a ghost omen? Perhaps what the omen had been wearing, the blood on his hands, had been warning signs for Bethan all along. It meant that some day, before he got too much older, Jay was going to die. But what it also meant was that day wasn't right now.

"So I'm just back to knowing I might die one day soon, but not what I'll be wearing," Jay said. "That's put an end to my crossing roads without looking and kissing girls career."

"I think I know why the messages are always so muddled," Hashim said, looking up at the clock. Bethan's parents had gone through already to be at her side. "I think that for active spirits, the sort of ghosts who try and change things here in this world, it's like fighting through a fog, or talking on a mobile with terrible reception. They have to try so hard to get through at all – even here in Weirdsville – that it takes most of their energy. They don't mean to be cryptic, they just have to be."

"That message we saw at your house," Jay said, thinking of the words that were scratched into the paint. "That wasn't cryptic."

"It must have been for Bethan," Kelly said, looking over at the doorway. Any minute now they would know.

"Perhaps, or perhaps it's for someone else?" Jay said. "Whatever happens I've got a feeling it's going to get a lot scarier and a lot more dangerous before it's over."

The four of them fell into an uneasy silence as they waited in the hospital visitors' room.

Bethan had lost so much blood that by the time the ambulance crew arrived her heart had stopped beating. Quickly and expertly, they had worked until they got a pulse again, stemming the bleeding, pumping air into her lungs to try and protect against brain damage, and putting her on a plasma drip. They saved her life, but until now, no one was quite sure for how long. Bethan had been on the point of major organ failure and the doctors took the decision to put her on a heart bypass machine and life support, putting her into a deep medical coma to allow her body to rest. Kelly had overheard the surgeon telling Bethan's mum that it was risky, but the only chance that Bethan had. They were here today because the doctors were taking Bethan off life support.

At first the Carpenters had made it very clear they didn't want Kelly, Jay or Hashim and especially Charlotte anywhere near their daughter. But the friends kept coming every day anyway, at first sitting outside the hospital waiting for one or other of Bethan's parents to walk by, braving their hurt and anger to find out how she was. And then in the hospital café, every minute they could get away from school and some when they shouldn't. Finally Bethan's mother had come over to where they were sitting.

"I don't know what you got my daughter involved in, but I can see that you care about her. You can wait with us."

It seemed like Bethan's parents had been gone for a very long time. Kelly's fingers were firmly entwined in Jay's, Hashim was sitting on the other side of her, wishing he had the courage to take her other hand.

Bethan's mum came into the room, tears streaming down her face.

"No!" Kelly stood up, as Mrs Carpenter came towards them.

"She's breathing," Bethan's mum beamed through her tears. "Her heart's working fine and she's breathing and... they said it might be hours before she came round, but she opened her eyes almost straightaway! The doctors have never seen anything like it. She can barely talk, the tubes made her throat very sore – but she wants to see you..."

Jay stood up, his heart beating hard at the thought of seeing Bethan – he'd been more frightened that he might lose her than he realised.

"You've got five minutes." Bethan's mum's smile faded. "I'm letting you see her because it's what she wants and I don't want her upset. But once she's home, once she's better, none of you are ever seeing her again, do you understand?"

Bethan's eyes were shut as she lay quietly in the darkened room, a stern-looking nurse watching over her readings. Kelly sat beside her on the bed and held her hand.

"Bethan, Beth," she whispered. "We're here."

Bethan's eyes flickered open, her mouth working for a moment before she managed to croak one word. "Jay?"

"Yes, I'm here." Jay stepped forward. "You haven't got rid of me yet."

The faintest of smiles cracked her dry lips.

"Kelly," she said, just loud enough to hear, every word barely more than a struggled rasp. "I... died."

"No, you're alive, there's a heart monitor and everything to prove it," Kelly reassured her.

"No," Bethan wheezed between each laboured word. "Heart stopped. I… was… dead. I… saw Tara, the girls and… many souls, so many." She coughed painfully, and Kelly could see Bethan's mum hovering beyond the doorway, desperate to be back by her daughter's side.

"Suffering." Bethan paused, the nurse was keeping a close eye on her heart-rate which had picked up.

"Here." Kelly lifted a cup of ice chips to Bethan's lips and waited while they melted in her mouth.

"Kelly, I saw her." Bethan grasped Kelly's wrist. "I saw your mother… She was crying. Oh, Kelly… your mum needs your help."